ROAR LIKE A
GIRL

Library of Congress Cataloging-in-Publication Data
is available.
Library of Congress Catalog Card Number on file

ISBN 978-1-939775-07-8

16 15 14 13 12   1 2 3 4 5 6 7 8 9 10

Little Pickle Press, Inc.
3701 Sacramento Street #494
San Francisco, CA 94118

Please visit us at www.littlepicklepress.com

ROAR LIKE A GIRL

Coleen Murtagh Paratore

Other books by Coleen Murtagh Paratore:

FIREFLIES: A Writer's Notebook
Writing it Right
BIG
Dreamsleeves
Sunny Holiday
Sweet and Sunny
The Wedding Planner's Daughter
The Cupid Chronicles
Willa by Heart
Forget Me Not
Wish I Might
From Willa, With Love
Mack McGinn's Big Win
The Funeral Director's Son
Kip Campbell's Gift
A Pearl Among Princes
Catching the Sun
How Prudence Proovit Proved the Truth about Fairy Tales
26 Big Things Small Hands Do

Visit the author at: *www.coleenparatore.com*

To every girl,
everywhere,
ROAR.
> —Cheering for you always,
> ***Coleen*** ☺

CONTENTS

Bramble

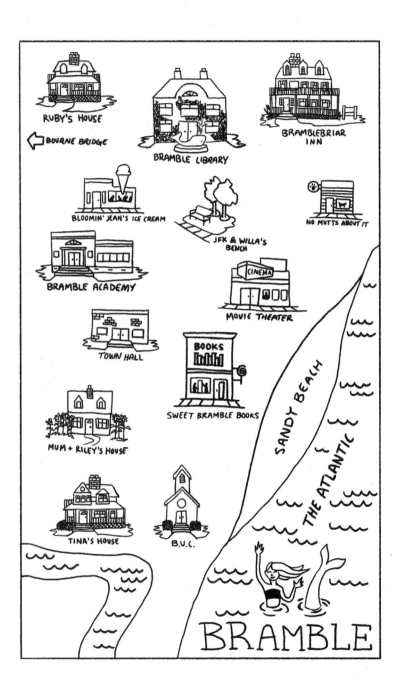

Chapter 1
A Golden Bubble

Change in all things is sweet.
—Aristotle

"I love my life." The words leap out as I bike away from the Inn. Does a person have the right to be this happy? It's as if I am floating in a golden bubble.

I love my family—Mom, Sam, Nana, Salty Dog, my new-found half-brother, Will. I love my home, the Bramblebriar Inn, with its beautiful old beams and full-to-the-brim library. I love my friends and classmates, all my teachers at Bramble Academy. I love living on Cape Cod, Massachusetts, where I can run down to the ocean and spend time with the waves whenever I want. I love our sweet, small town of Bramble and all the amazing people I've grown close to, like Sulamina Mum, Mrs. Saperstone, Dr. Swaminathan. And, of course, Joseph Francis Kennelly, "JFK," my boyfriend.

I grin and bike faster.

I call him Joseph or Joey, but I secretly think of him by the initials he shares with that famous JFK, President John Fitzgerald Kennedy—the "Ask not what your country can do for you, ask what *you* can do for your country" one. He loved Cape Cod, too.

My JFK has been in Florida at a baseball camp all summer. We had a glitch in our relationship. He began hanging out with a girl down there—Lorna—and I had feelings for another Bramble boy: the quiet and mysterious Jess Farrelly—long wavy hair, dreamy brown eyes, leather rope choker; and drummer in a local band. I worked myself into such a foggy conundrum—JFK or Jessie? JFK or Jessie?—that I decided to take a break from boys.

But then I kept listening to the song JFK wrote for me, about our first date. I was at home with a broken foot, feeling awful because I couldn't go to the Valentine's dance at school, when JFK showed up in a tux. I put on the dress I'd purchased for the dance, bunny slippers instead of heels, and we danced. That was the night he gave me the heart-shaped locket.

I touch it now, back on my neck where it belongs. I can't believe that I'd ever wanted a break from JFK. He was always doing kind things for me, like the song, or for complete strangers, like the time he'd spent hours helping a woman find her car. He is the guy for me. I am sure now.

I texted Jessie last night to tell him, officially, but things have been cooling off for a few weeks now. Jessie has a lot going on in his family right now, and a confused Willa isn't high on his priority list. He sent back a sweet *No worries, Willa*. I promise myself that after a week or two I'll check in on him. Friends stick together, even after awkward breakups.

Pedaling along, I take a deep breath and clear my head. It is a postcard-perfect sunny day, late August, with that first exciting hint of autumn in the air, a spicy wisp of change. All four seasons on Cape are sublime, but fall is my favorite. The first day of school in September always feels like New Year's Day. Who knows what surprises lie ahead? The possibilities are endless.

I'm about to start 10th grade at Bramble Academy. I'm really looking forward to being a sophomore. Last year, I played soccer and ran track, but I'm thinking about branching out this year—maybe now is the time to try my hand at music. I want this year to be the best yet.

I'm also thinking of running for class president. I have some experience: I was community service leader last year, and my classmates said I did a good job. I know class president is a big responsibility, but I think I'm up for it. Plus, Bramble Academy has *never had a girl class president,* which is unacceptable. Why not me?

I'm trying to pay more attention to national politics this year. Right now, President Obama and his family are vacationing on Martha's Vineyard, an island off the Cape coast. They visit every August. I think he's doing a good job as commander in chief, and I like how First Lady Michelle got healthier foods into schools. Their daughters are about my age. *What would it be like to be the daughter of a president?* I keep pedaling as I imagine.

I pass Sweet Bramble Books and wave to my Nana. She runs the half-book, half-candy store, my favorite place in town. I'm glad to see it full of customers today. Maybe if I wrote a letter, the Obamas would visit our store next summer. We're just a quick ferry ride from the Vineyard. Nana drew a huge crowd when James Taylor, the famous singer, signed his new book at her store. Big names draw customers. These few precious months of high-tourist season keep Nana in business all year and keep me, her only grandchild, very, very content. When you are a girl who devours books like candy and candy like, well, *candy*, you can't get any luckier than having Sweet Bramble Books in your family.

Biking through town brings even more memories of JFK. There's Bloomin' Jean's ice cream, where he always gets mint chocolate chip and I get Heath Bar Crunch vanilla frozen yogurt. Next, I see the library and the whale-spoutin' fountain. It makes me think of the times JFK tags along while I browse the shelves. He pretends not to be interested, but soon he checks out even more books than I do. And there's the bench where JFK and I often sit together; the bench where I've begun leaving copies of treasured books from my personal library with the note:

> *Take me home, free, if you wish to read,*
> *Then when you're finished, replant the seed.*
> *Leave me somewhere for a new friend to find.*
> *A book is a perennial thing. It blooms on and on.*
> *From Cape Cod, With Love,*
> *Willa Havisham*

I love my books and giving them up was hard at first. But then I thought about the comfort they bring me, and I knew someone else might need them even more. The first book I placed there was *Anne of Green Gables*, one of my dearest literary friends. I wonder who is enjoying it now? Hopefully, Anne's antics bring a smile to their face and brighten their day. Straddling my bike, I reach into to my basket, lift out my next gift, *Little Women*. No matter who picks it up, Jo March will have a thing or two to teach them. "See ya later, Jo!" I wave goodbye as I bike off.

I stop for pedestrians at a crosswalk near the new day spa. Right then, the door of the spa opens and out comes Tina Belle, my on-and-off best friend, and Ruby Sivler, who's usually a royal pain in the butt, but I'm trying to talk to her more this summer. Ruby's mom, Mrs. Sivler, has breast cancer, and it's hard to be mad at someone going through that. Ruby and Tina spend a lot of time together, which leaves me a little out of the loop. I was hanging out with my friend, Mariel Sanchez, but this summer she's in New York City visiting her actress mother. That leaves me without a resident best friend, but I'm happy for Mariel.

"Still wearing those pink sneakers, huh?" Ruby stares at my feet. She and Tina are wearing matching gold gladiator sandals that show off their freshly pedicured green toenails.

Ruby still loves to tease me about my pink Chucks. When I saw them in the window of Lammers' clothing store, I walked right in and bought them. I even wore them out of the store. They're my favorite thing in my closet.

"Nice green color," I say.

"It's a transitional shade," Tina explains.

"Plus, it totally sets off the gold, right?" Ruby adds.

"Sure!" I'm not much into fashion, but Ruby and Tina live for it, so I try to at least listen. I smile. "I'm off to the beach. See you later!"

"Willa, wait," Tina says. "Our book is finished—we have printed copies! It turned out really well."

Ruby and Tina are the "authors" of *The Beach Boys of Cape Cod*, a guide to the Cape beaches with the hottest college lifeguards—guys posing on surfboards or on lifeguard chairs —with captions describing a few of their "favorite things"—foods, teams, places to take dates. It required weeks of research…really in-depth questions and analysis. Ruby's dad paid to have the book published.

"We're having a book launch party on Sunday at the Popponesset Inn at 6:00 p.m.," Tina says. "Please come, okay? And bring Mariel if she's back from New York and Joey if he's back from Florida. Gosh, it's like everyone cleared out of Bramble this summer." She stops smiling, a cloud passes over her pretty face, but she brightens almost immediately. "But the launch is a great excuse to get everyone together!"

"Come on, Tina," Ruby says. "We've got to pack. Your dad said we're leaving for the airport at three o'clock, and I still haven't packed my shoes."

"Aren't you only going for the weekend?" I ask.

Tina looks at me. I know she feels bad, not wanting me to be hurt that the Belles are taking Ruby with them on their annual August trip to Saratoga, New York. "I'm not really in to going this year," Tina says to me. "Not with our book launch and all. My dad's excited because he's a new part-owner of a horse that's running in the Travers Stakes. It won't win, of course. Triple Crown winner American Pharoah's got that trophy in the bag."

Wow, Tina's never been interested in horse races before. Maybe I've missed more than I thought. I make a mental note to try and connect with Tina more often this school year. "What's your dad's horse's name?"

"Keen Ice."

"Keen Ice. Sounds like a winning name to me." I remember how Mr. Belle patiently explained to me the nuances of picking horses to win, place, and show. I got the idea for my "Willa's Pix" from the "Kid's Pix" sheets they hand out at the entrance to the track. I reach in my pack for some money. "Here, Tina. Put two dollars on Keen Ice to win for me, okay?"

"To win?" Tina laughs. "Oh, he doesn't have a prayer of beating the Pharoah. How about I bet him to show? Even that would be a long shot."

"Oh, come on, Tina, have a little faith. He might surprise you." She takes the money. "Okay, Willa, whatever."

"Have fun in Saratoga! I'll see you Sunday."

I hop on my bike and keep going down Main Street. I love checking out all my favorite places, remembering things that have happened all over this wonderful town. At the other end of Main Street is BUC, Bramble United Community, "a home for every heart," where my beloved friend Sulimina Mum is minister. Mum is also going through treatment for breast cancer. I couldn't believe it when I'd first heard the news. I was so worried that I couldn't even think straight for weeks. But Mum, the one I'm supposed to be comforting, came to my rescue. She said she refuses to be discouraged. She's fighting cancer with "spirit and a smile." Mum was my first friend in Bramble. She's taught me volumes about life, about not worrying and about working to help others, instead of focusing on myself.

I can't believe it's been only two years since Mom and I moved to Cape Cod. When our car crested the top of that roller-coaster-like Bourne Bridge, connecting the mainland to the peninsula, white caps sparkling on the waves below, I opened the window, and the wind whooshed in, "welcome, Willa, welcome home." In that moment, I prayed that, after years of moving, maybe, finally, this would be "home" forever.

For as long as I can remember, my mom has moved us to a new city every few years. My dad died before I was born, and Nana said Mom loved him too much to imagine a home without him. Whenever someone got too close, or too serious, she'd pack up her business, Weddings by Havisham—and my life—and we'd end up in a new city within the week. I hated always being the new girl, never having friends for more than a school year or two.

Then one day, my nana convinced Mom to come home to Bramble, Cape Cod, where my mom grew up, and, somehow, lucky starfish, Mom agreed. It's been one amazing thing after another since then. Mom met Sam—our next door neighbor and my English teacher— and she finally opened her heart. They got married last year, and it's been wonderful to see Mom—and Sam—so happy. Recently, I've started calling him Dad, which always makes us smile.

And Mom's business is doing great, too! Sam's grandmother left him her estate, right on the Cape. We spent our first year as a family renovating the property into the Bramblebriar Inn. It's now one of the finest destination hotels on Cape Cod. There's a two-year waiting list for one of my mom's signature weddings here.

I pull myself out of reminiscing and into the present—before I miss my beach turn-off. I need my ocean time. I turn off the road, lock my bike, and untie my pink Chucks. Standing at the top of the weathered gray stairs, I rest my hands on the wooden railing and soak in the scene before me: the ocean, boats, people sunbathing, families lounging beneath umbrellas, lots of folks reading, kids tossing footballs, children building sandcastles—

"Come on guys, keep up," says a tourist dad heading my way. You can always tell a tourist by the lobster-red sunburn and Cuffy's t-shirt. He's hauling a wagon loaded with a cooler, chairs, and floats. Two young girls, carrying towels and toys, are struggling to keep pace. I bet the mom is already ahead of them, scouting out a good spot on the beach.

I smile and close my eyes. I take a deep breath and let it go. Warm sun on my face, breeze blowing my hair, the sound of waves lapping against the shore, the smell of coconut lotion....

Thank you, God, for this wonderful life.

Chapter 2
What Does Your Name Stand For?

One child, one teacher, one book, one pen can change the world.

—Malala Yousafzai

I unroll my beach blanket and take out my lunch, a tuna sandwich on wheat, dill pickle, nectarine, Cape Cod chips, and two spice cookies made with zucchini from Sam's garden. Mom manages the Inn and staff, handles all the weddings, and pays the bills. Sam oversees the kitchen as well as the vegetable and flower gardens. He gave up his teaching post at Bramble Academy to help Mom run the Inn, but I think he misses teaching, and I know he misses writing.

The beach is less crowded than last week; already the tourists are saying goodbye to Cape Cod and returning home. After Labor Day, if I get here early, I can have the whole beach to myself. I slather on sunscreen and stretch out on my stomach to read. Last night I finished *The Hunger Games*. Even though Katniss makes a great addition to my literary collection of strong, independent women, I'm ready for something a bit different. Today I'm starting *I Am Malala*, which Dr. Swaminathan says I absolutely must read.

It's the true story of Malala Yousafzai of Pakistan. She was only fifteen, a few months older than I am, when the Taliban boarded her school bus and shot her at point-blank range in the head for speaking out for a girl's right to attend school in her country, just like boys can. Malala's photograph is on the jacket. Her stunning brown eyes stare out at me. This girl has something to say.

The book lures me in immediately. I read for two hours until I get sleepy. I mark my place and close my eyes. This is my first day off in a long time. Summer is our busiest season at the Inn, and I waitress every day, as well as help out Nana at the store. Thankfully, as of check-out today, Mom didn't book any guests for the rest of the week. She's having all the rugs and draperies cleaned in preparation for the Kardellian wedding this weekend. That gives me two whole days to spend with JFK!

When I wake up, I make my way toward the water. Even on a hot August day like this, the ocean is chilly but refreshing. I dive under, surface and swim, then lie on my back and let the water carry my weight, rocking me like a baby.

Back at my blanket, I towel dry, open my beach bag for my water and bag of candy—salt-water taffy and mint juleps—sticky but yummy nonetheless. I fish out a pen and my journal, which is nearly full; time to buy a new one. My Gramp Tweed, deceased now, but forever with me in spirit, gave me my first blank book—it was brown with a yellow sunflower on the cover. Gramp and I would sit on the couch and drink lemon tea and "book talk." He said to read the best books while I'm young. Gramp was sure I'd be an author someday. He said the secret to writing is to "tell the truth and put your heart into it" and that anyone could write his or her own story. I've been writing about my life ever since. In my bedroom bookcase, there's a whole row of journals in chronological order.

As always, when the pen strikes the page, my worries pour out first. *Should I tell JFK I kissed Jessie that night? It was just one quick kiss. I don't think I should tell him, though. It didn't mean anything, and I've told Jessie....*

"What are you writing?" someone asks.

I look up to see a young girl smiling at me. She's wearing a striking orange bathing suit, the color glowing neon bright against her beautiful skin, matching orange clips on her braids, orange sunglasses, and flip-flops. She's clutching a notebook with pink, orange, and yellow smiley faces. Her sunny persona demands a smile in return.

"Hi." I close my journal and sit up. "I'm just writing about my life."

"Oh." She lifts her over-sized sunglasses so we can see eyes to eyes. "That's nice. My name's Mikaela. What's yours?"

"Nice to meet you, Mikaela. I'm Willa." We shake hands. "Are you here on vacation?"

Mikaela nods. "We come here every year. That's my mom over there under the umbrella." Mikaela's mother sees her pointing. We smile and wave to one another.

"What are you writing?" I ask, nodding at Mikaela's notebook.

"An acrostic poem about my name. Want to see?"

"Sure. Here, sit down." I clear a spot on my blanket.

We look at what she's written.

M *usical.* "I'm a really good singer."

I *ce Cream Maker.* "My Auntie Shelly bought me an ice-cream maker for my birthday. I'm nine now. I set up a neighborhood ice-cream stand in our driveway. I do one flavor a day. So far, strawberry cheesecake was the best. I'm the first entrepreneur in my family."

"Good for you. That's impressive." I look back at her poem.

K itten Mama. I tap the photo taped onto the page. "Who are these cuties?"

Mikaela laughs. "That's Lilly and Bro. They're so much fun. We got them at the shelter. My cousin Kyleigh is kitty-sitting them for me. Do you have pets?"

"Yes. A big furry-bear golden retriever named Salty Dog. He gets stinky rolling around in fishy stuff on the beach, but I love him. He smiles like a person." I try to demonstrate.

Mikaela giggles. "You're funny, Willa. Can I see Salty Dog? Where is he?"

"He's home, probably taking a nap."

"Where's home?"

"Here in town. We run the Bramblebriar Inn."

"You live here on Cape Cod?" Mikaela's eyes widen. "I love it here. I wish we could stay forever."

"Mikaela!" her mother calls over to her. "Come on, babe, time for lunch."

"Okay, Mom! I've got to go, Willa. It was nice meeting you."

"You, too, Mikaela. Good luck with your ice-cream business. Maybe I'll see you here next year."

"Okay. Bye." She walks, then turns back. "Hey, wait. What does your name stand for? If you did an acrostic poem for Willa, what would the words be?"

"I'll think about that." I smile. "I'll tell you next summer, okay?"

*****

Mom and Sam and I go to Wimpy's in Osterville for dinner. I think they have the best fish and chips on the whole Cape. Sam disagrees, but I'm determined to bring him over to my side. I order a cup of clam chowder to start. Mom and Sam get salads. We take our time deciding on main courses. It's nice having an evening together away from the Inn, but Mom's phone keeps beeping and she needs to read her messages.

"I'm sorry," she sighs loudly. "This is important. I'll be right back." She leaves the table, walks outside the restaurant. I see her face in the street light, talking then listening, listening. She looks exhausted, unhappy. I notice that Sam is watching her, too. We look at each other. He smiles and winks. "Willa, come on, eat your chowder before it gets cold."

When Mom returns, she apologizes. She picks at her salad, pushes the plate away.

"What's wrong, babe?" Sam asks, putting his hand on her arm.

"I'm tired, Sam. I used to love planning weddings, but it isn't fun anymore. These brides keep getting more demanding. I'm losing my patience. It's hard to keep from snapping their heads off, and that would be really bad for business."

The waitress brings our entrees. Grilled salmon for Mom, a lobster roll for Sam, good old-fashioned Cape Cod fish 'n' chips for me. Sam changes the subject. "There are some good movies out. Maybe we can see one tomorrow night."

"Sure, maybe," Mom says.

I nod along, not really paying attention. The only movie I want to see is the one in which Willa and JFK are reunited after six weeks apart and do a lot of kissing.

Back home, I continue reading *I Am Malala*. There's only one blank page left in my journal. I read over what I wrote on the beach, smiling as I think of that sunny little sprite, Mikaela. "What does your name stand for Willa?"

Hmm...let's see. I write:

W edding planner

I ntelligent (at least I think so)

L oves JFK

L ibrary Saver (I once helped keep the Bramble Library from closing.)

A ... nxious for tomorrow to get here already. I can't wait to see JFK!

Chapter 3
Pink Feats Forward

If you don't like something, change it. If you can't
change it, change your attitude.

—Maya Angelou

It's nearly 8:00 a.m. when I wake. Sunlight is streaming in through the jar of beach glass and jingle shells on my windowsill, painting tiny, dancing rainbows—green, blue, brown, orange, and yellow—on my wall. I sit up in bed and turn on the TV to check the weather.

"Thanks, guys," a woman says to anchors Matt Lauer and Savannah Guthrie. Matt Lauer is a guy, but Savannah Guthrie is clearly not. Why do people say "guys" when there are girls in the group, too? "Come on guys, keep up," that dad said to his little daughters on the beach yesterday. The local weather comes on. "Another beautiful day, high in the mid-eighties."

The Inn phone rings. I hear Sam answer, call out that it's for my mom. Salty Dog barks outside my door. "Come on, buddy," Sam says, clearly trying to tempt him away from my room. "Let's get you outside." I open my door and give Salty a big hug. "You go ahead with Sam this morning, Salty. I want to go a bit faster today. I'll see both of you later. Love you!"

As I dress for a run, I look over at the poster from the Falmouth Road Race. Mom and I ran it together. She was so excited when our names got picked in the lottery; it's a very popular event. This year there were 12,000 runners. It's a seven-mile course, from Woods Hole to the beach in Falmouth Heights. We trained for months. Mom's faster than I am, and she races a lot, but she kept pace with me, both in training and at the race. I knew her competitive side wanted to run ahead, but she said she'd rather run with her daughter. I ran well, about a ten-minute mile— I'm shooting for a nine next year. I'm glad Mom and I found something we can enjoy doing together. But not today. Sometimes it's nice to run alone with your thoughts.

I run a loop around the neighborhood, an easy three miles, do some sit-ups and pushups on the front lawn, then head into the kitchen for breakfast. Our new baker, Coby Mabitu, has the morning off; otherwise, I'd be smelling fresh-baked peach muffins or a raspberry strudel. Looking out the window, I see Salty and Sam in the garden. Mom's working at the kitchen table. She gives me a quick wave and rolls her eyes, indicating a bride-to-be is giving her a hard time about something. I smile and nod sympathetically, thinking about what she shared last night.

I pour orange juice, toast a bagel and coat it with honey-nut cream cheese, and grab a banana to take up to my room. If I hang around too long, Mom will give me a list of chores. All I want to do is eat, shower, relax, do my hair, and take my time to decide what to wear. JFK texted me yesterday, asking me to meet him at two o'clock in town at the bench by Bloomin' Jeans. I was surprised he didn't want to go to the beach or go sailing or see a movie, but we can make a plan when we meet. His mother, Mrs. Kennelly, said he got a buzz cut because it was so hot in Florida. I bet it looks hot on him, not that he could get much cuter. He is definitely the most handsome boy in Bramble—sea blue eyes, dimple to die for, a smile that takes your breath away, beautiful inside and out.

I set my breakfast on my desk and turn on CNN. There are about a dozen men and one woman all jockeying to get the nomination as the Republican Party candidate for president in 2016. They are talking about immigration and securing the borders. Former Secretary of State Hillary Clinton is the top candidate on the Democratic side. I wonder if our country will finally elect a woman president? Mother and Sam have lively discussions about politics. Mom is a registered Republican; Sam is registered Democrat. I'm not registered anything because you can't vote until you're 18, which doesn't seem fair—teens should be able to vote. I hear people say that young people aren't involved. Well, maybe that's because they don't feel like anyone's listening. I know I'd vote if someone gave me the chance.

When I first volunteered to be community service leader for our class, I asked our minister, Sulamina Mum, for ideas. She said there are lots of ways to make a difference, but if I picked a cause I really cared about, something close to my heart, then I would surely succeed.

I took Mum's advice to heart and focused on things I care about. I helped save the Bramble Library. They were losing funding, and it was about to close—we couldn't have that! I helped raise money and got people involved, and now when I see little girls going in the library, I am so proud I was a part of saving it. That lead to all sorts of projects: raising money for affordable housing; initiating green recycling campaigns; and now the "Perennial Library," leaving books on that Bramble bench for other readers to enjoy and pass along. My Nana says we are lucky ducks— we have our health, home, and a happy family—and that when you've got a lot, you should give a lot. Sam calls it paying your "community rent," that is, giving a portion of your time, talent, or treasure (by which he means money) to make a difference.

JFK pays his community rent, too. He volunteers at the homeless shelter in Hyannis with his mom. Yet another reason why he is the perfect guy for me.

I choose a white tank top and pink shorts that match my sneakers. I'm wearing pink proudly now. In the past, I was unfair to the color. But when I saw these pink Chucks, it was love at first blink. *Pink*. This year, I will be a girl on the go, putting my best feats, my best *pink* feats forward.

My hair has gotten longer and blonder from the sun. I work styling cream through it and scrunch handfuls into soft curls. When it dries, I smooth on some Moroccan oil. I try to picture JFK in a buzz cut. I imagine it feels fuzzy. Can't wait to find out.

I put on some foundation, eyeliner, mascara, blush, pink lipstick, a spritz of perfume… the locket and silver hoop earrings.

On one of our first phone calls of the summer, JFK explained that he was spending a lot of time with his grandparents at their country club, which was really boring—there was "nobody our age" except this girl,

Lorna. They played tennis, "no big deal." I wondered though, and when I didn't hear from him for four days, and then got a strange call from Lorna asking what kind of cake Joey liked best because she was throwing a surprise birthday party for him…well…. And while all of this Florida-Lorna drama was going on, Jessie started talking to me…he with those dreamy-sad eyes, smelling like the sun and spice cologne…inviting me to come hear his band….

JFK! JFK! JFK! my mind chants, unable to focus on anything else.

Finally, it's time for me to head toward town. I bike through the streets, maneuvering around the last tourists of the summer. Even with their dwindling numbers, they're still crowding the streets and traffic makes it slow going. *Please get out of my way,* I want to shout, wishing I had a horn to *beep.* Finally, I see JFK, sitting on our bench, his bike propped against a tree. He's wearing blue and yellow madras shorts and a blue polo shirt, head down looking at his iPhone.

"Joseph!" I call out. I can't get off my bike and in his arms fast enough.

But when he looks up, he's not the smiling boy I've been imagining. There's a strange coldness in his eyes. "You were *kissing* him, Willa," he spits out.

I stop short. A million words spring to my lips, apologies, excuses, but all I can get out "Wh-what?" I stand there awkwardly, wanting to sit down next to him but also hyper-aware of the anger coming off him in waves. I stare at him, noting all the changes from the summer. It's only been a few months, but he seems older, changed somehow. The buzz cut makes his harsh expression even harsher. His arms are folded across his chest and his jaw is set in a hard line.

"You send me a lame note saying you 'need some time and just want to be *friends*.'" Every word comes out like a punch to my gut. "The truth is you've been cheating on me."

"Joey, no." My body unfreezes and I sit down next to him. "Listen…." Heart pounding, hand shaking, I reach out to touch his shoulder.

"Don't lie, Willa." He pulls away. "The proof's here." He holds up his phone. "Look!"

He shoves his phone into my hands, and I scroll through a series of pictures: Jessie and me on the beach; Jessie leaning down to whisper in my ear; me with my arms around his neck, on tip-toe to kiss him.

"Really, Willa?" JFK says. "Drummer-head Jessie?"

Something about the way he says it makes me livid. "What's that supposed to mean? You're upset that I kissed someone you don't deem *good* enough?" My hands are clenched on my knees now, and I can feel myself shaking.

JFK keeps talking. "He's a jerk, Willa. And he runs like a girl. And you *kissed* him."

I can't believe what I'm hearing. "*Runs like a girl?*" How could one summer have changed my sweet boyfriend into…this. "Joey, that's a horrible thing to say."

"When did you become such a feminist?" he asks, looking at me like I'm a complete stranger.

"I've always been a feminist! When did you become such a…," I search for the right words.

He glares at me. "Don't change the subject, Willa. You know what this is about. What were you thinking?"

"It wasn't anything." My emotions are so jumbled; I can barely hold back the tears. I can't believe this is happening.

"How could you do this to me?" JFK slumps down on the bench.

"It…it didn't mean anything, Joey. It's nothing. I don't care about…him, I care about you. Joey, please.…"

He folds his arms across his chest again, blocking me out.

We sit there in silence.

A happy couple walks out of Bloomin' Jean's. "Why don't we get some ice cream," I suggest. "We can talk more about this later."

I put my hand on his knee.

He flinches. "Don't touch me."

My body turns cold. "Joey." His name comes out in a sob.

"Willa," he looks up at me and I can see the hurt all over his face. "I can't." His eyes land on the heart locket nestled over my heart. Memories flicker across his face. "I can't trust you anymore."

"Joseph, listen." My heart is pounding, but I try to stay calm. "Jessie was so upset that night…his parents are divorcing…he may have to move. I was listening and being a friend."

"No, Willa. A hug is being a friend. A *kiss* is being a girlfriend."

"I'm not his girlfriend!"

"You're not mine, either."

JFK stands abruptly, shoves my bike off of his, the metal rims clattering against the sidewalk. He gets on and starts to pedal.

"Joseph, please, wait!"

Then quick as a blink, he's gone.

Knees weak, shaking, I sink down on the bench.

So this is what it feels like when your heart breaks.

Chapter 4
Rosie the Riveter

*Things change…things happen…things you can't
even imagine when you're young and full of hope.*
—Judy Blume

Nose dripping, mascara running down my cheeks, I bike to the beach, lock my bike, toss off my Chucks, and hurry down the steps to the water. Stomach heaving, head and heart in a storm—when I am this sad or mad or both, only the ocean can heal.

It's cloudy now, and the beach is clearing out, a few clusters of people are all that's left. Kids shriek as the tide comes in. The waves fill the moat channels around their sandcastles, and then melt and sweep their creations out to sea. I head out in the opposite direction of where Jess and I walked that night. *What was I thinking?* I wasn't thinking. It was purely an emotional thing. I felt sorry for him about his parents. And, to be honest, I had feelings for him. I was curious. In the moment though, it was a spontaneous thing. I didn't plan to cheat on JFK. Is one kiss cheating?

JFK and I were a couple for two years. Doesn't that mean anything? And what about him and Lorna? No one snuck around snapping shots of them. I kick a conch shell out of the way.

How can JFK throw us away so easily? How can he end us over one mistake? He wouldn't even listen to me. He's acting all tough and hardened as if he went to military boot camp instead of sports camp.

Run like a girl. What a stupid thing to say. I pick up a green plastic pail and fling it up on the beach grass, safely past the tide line, in case the little owner comes back looking for it.

JFK, how could you turn on me so quickly? Not even giving us a chance to talk. I don't deserve to be treated like this. Clearly you're not at all the boy I built you up to be. Puffing out your chest, shouting at me, biking off mad like you lost a baseball game instead of your girlfriend.

Grow up.

On and on I walk, alternating between sad and mad, heartbroken and furious, talking it all out. The wonderful thing about the ocean is that as noisy and wild as it is sometimes, it always *always* listens. It sweeps in and out, no words, no questions, no "why's" or wise advice. The ocean just listens, listens, listens. *Let it go, Willa, let it go.*

By the time I reach home, it's dark. Turning onto our street, I'm comforted by the sight of our beautiful inn, the warm lights welcoming me. I pause for a moment to take it all in: the grand white colonial, green shutters, brick chimneys; the wide wrap-around porch with comfy wicker couches and chairs, hanging baskets of red and white geraniums, blue hydrangea in full bloom, countless tiny white twinkle lights; and beyond the main inn, the guest houses, vegetable and perennial gardens, fruit trees, the labyrinth, the tire swings and seesaw, the hammocks, the rose garden and arbor—a favorite place for wedding vows—the converted barn where my friends and I held dances to save the Bramble Library, the Adirondack chairs and peddle-boats by the pond, the blue lights illuminating the new fountain installed especially for this Saturday's wedding.

A cool breeze sets the wind chimes to music and reminds me that fall is coming. My gaze settles on the statue of the girl lying on her stomach reading, the gift Mom and Sam brought me back from Nantucket when they eloped. The girl is lounging beneath the cherry tree I planted two years ago. *When life throws you a pit, plant a cherry tree.*

I head into the house. My stomach is rumbling, but I can't eat right now. All I want is to hug my giant furry teddy bear of a dog.

Salty's not waiting for me on the porch. He's not in the foyer on the rug by the grandfather clock. There's a note from my mom on the registration desk. "At a meeting. Be back late. Salty is at the spa overnight. He stunk horribly. I ordered the full treatment."

Just when I need my dog the most. I must admit, though, Salty is extra stinky, a combination of sweating in the summer heat and rolling around on the beach. He's like a cat-dog; he loves fish so much. No Mutts

About It, the poshy pet spa across the street, is owned by Ruby Sivler's family. Perhaps some pets like pampering—the spa even does *pawdicures*, "parent's choice of polish"—but that would be my poor Salty's idea of a nightmare.

Unfortunately, Salty's feelings come second to any bride's. There's a big wedding this weekend, and smelly dogs aren't good for business. No one wants a wedding that reeks of fish, no matter how cute the dog. *Sorry, Salty.*

Early Friday morning, our staff will make up the beds with all new 800-count luxury bed linens Mom purchased, then add the special welcoming touches the bride ordered for her guests' rooms: thick terry-cloth bathrobes and slippers, scented soaps, oils and lotions, gift baskets filled with bottles of sparkling water, juices, wine, and all-natural organic Cape Cod foods, like our specialty cheeses and dark-chocolate-covered cranberries. They sound delicious, but expensive. If I ran a wedding planning business, I'd have the whole event cost less than a thousand. I might even shoot for a $100 wedding—Willa's Wonderful One-hundred-dollar Weddings.

"Willa, is that you?" Sam calls to me from the library.

He is reading the newspaper, sitting in one of the expensive wing back chairs with matching ottomans Mom bought when she remodeled the Inn.

"Hi, Dad." I sink down on the ottoman.

Sam studies my face. He puts the paper aside. "You look like you need someone to talk to."

"Guys can be real jerks."

Sam nods. "We certainly can."

I laugh. "Not you, of course." I tell him some of what happened with JFK. "He actually said Jessie *runs like a girl*...like that was a horrible insult." I leave out the kissing part.

"I guess he hasn't heard of Mo'ne Davis."

"Who?"

"The first girl—the first *player* ever—to pitch a shutout in the Little League World Series. She threw a seventy-mile-per-hour fastball at the age of thirteen. Mo'ne Davis has made 'throw like a girl' a compliment."

"Why wouldn't it be a compliment?"

"Coaches, *guy* coaches," Sam says, "will tell a player 'you're running like a girl' or 'you're throwing like a girl' to get them to be more aggressive."

"More macho, you mean?"

Sam nods and points at the newspaper. "I was just reading about National Women's Equality Day. Kristin Chenoweth, Cyndi Lauper, Sara Bareilles and other female entertainers posted tweets and Instagrams striking the classic Rosie the Riveter pose to call attention to the fact that we still don't have an Equal Rights Amendment in our country."

"What's the Equal Rights Amendment?"

"The Equal Rights Amendment is a proposed Amendment to the United States Constitution. It's to make sure everyone, regardless of gender, has equal rights and opportunities."

I think about this for a second. "Well, that seems like an obvious rule. What's the problem?"

"Congress passed the Equal Rights Amendment in the 1970's, but not enough states ratified it to become part of the Constitution," says Sam.

"Who would vote against equal rights for women?" I ask.

"Hmmm?" He looks up from his paper, his eyebrows furrowing even more as he sees my face. He puts his hand over mine. "What's wrong, Willa?"

"I just…I get confused sometimes. I mean, don't you ever feel like…." I start to pace around the study, trying to find the words. "Right now, I feel guilty for being upset over JFK when there's real stuff going on in the world, things like this—equality for women—or, the girls in Pakistan that I was reading about earlier. But at the same time…I already miss JFK and…." I feel my eyes start to well up with tears, so I take a deep breath. "Sometimes it feels like there's not enough room for me to feel both."

Sam gives me a small, kind smile. "That is a very good problem to have. It means you're a good person, Willa. It's normal. Not easy...." He holds up his hand when he sees I'm about to interrupt. "It's hard and, honestly, I've been trying to find a solution since I was about your age."

"You got one yet?" I ask, smiling weakly.

"No. Though I do know that it's not helpful to ignore the feelings—the personal or the global. Do your best to not get overwhelmed by them. Talk about it, do what you can, but remember that, while you are an extraordinary person, you are still only one person. It's not your responsibility to make everything all better right this second." He gives me a tight hug. "Enough about that," Sam says. "It's late. You must be hungry. Let me warm up—"

"No thanks, Dad. I'm going to lie down for a while. I'll grab something later."

"Okay." Sam hugs me again. "I love you, Willa."

"Love you, too, Dad."

*****

Upstairs, I lock my bedroom door. I can't deal with wedding to-do lists tonight. I wish Salty was here. *I hope you get spared a* pawdicure, *buddy.* He'll probably come back with "transitional green." I smile, thinking of Tina and Ruby.

Walking to my dresser, I gaze in the mirror. What a different reflection from earlier today when I was so excited getting ready to meet JFK. I unclasp the silver chain, open the heart. It has the two of us, separately, so that when I close it, we're kissing. It was just two years ago, but we both seem so young in the pictures. Especially Joey. I touch his face with my thumb for a second.

Tears blur our faces away. *Over, all over. Gone, all gone.* I toss the necklace in my jewelry box, collapse on my bed. Today's movie replays in my mind. It began so well....How could JFK have changed so much?

Chapter 5
Fireworks

It's never the changes we want that change everything.
—Junot Diaz

I'm awakened by the sound of fireworks. There are always celebrations during tourist season—anniversaries, birthdays, family reunions—often ending with a blast. I think of Salty Dog across the street at the spa. I hope he isn't too spooked. Salty is such a scaredy-cat about loud noises, fireworks, fire engines. I pull the comforter over my ears and doze off again.

In my dream, I'm trudging along the beach in the dark, every step an effort. The surf is pounding against the jetty, wind whipping against my face. "Willa!" someone calls. "Willa!—Willa!—" I turn to see. Maybe it's JFK—

"WILLA!!" someone is frantically shouting.

That's Sam's voice. I open my eyes, sit up, switch on the light.

I think my room is filled with fog, but I start coughing and realize it's smoke. *My entire room is filled with thick smoke.*

"Willa!" Sam is shaking me harder now, his voice harsh with panic. "There's a fire!
Hurry!"

I'm wide awake now. "Hurry, put your shoes on." He helps shove my feet into the pink Chucks, not bothering to tie them. "Come on." Sam takes my hand. The hallway is eerily lit, warm with smoke. "Keep your head down," he shouts.

"What happened? Where's Mom?"

"She's safe outside," he yells, then coughs.

Thank goodness Salty's at the spa.

There's a *whooshing* sound, and outside, sirens wailing. We stumble through the house, bent closer to the floor. The roaring gets louder. My eyes sting. The smoke thickens. I cough and gulp air. Sam ducks into a guest bathroom, grabs two towels, quickly holds them under a faucet, and runs back out.

"Here," he says, handing me one. "Breathe through this."

We reach the top of the stairs. A heat wave hits us. I look down. *Fire everywhere.*

"Sam!"

"Just keep walking, Willa," he says, his voice sturdy around me. "We can do this. Come on."

The banister is on fire. The smoke is horrible. A spark hits my hair and hisses.

Something crashes to the ground. Firefighters with masks and axes rush in the front door. The library off the lobby is engulfed in flames. *All of our books.*

"Anyone else in here?" a firefighter shouts.

"No!" Sam screams to be heard over the blaze. "The staff has the night off."

*My books. My journals. My...*I turn to go back. The smoke is so dense I can't breathe.

"No, Willa!" He tightens his grip on me. I try to pull away, but he throws me over his shoulder before I have time to react.

Cheers go up from the crowd. "They're safe!" someone shouts.

"Willa!" Mom screams, tears streaming down her face. She grabs me and Sam in a fierce hug. "Thank God, you're all right."

More firefighters jump out of a fire truck, adjusting masks and oxygen tanks, unfurling hoses, shouting orders, aiming powerful bursts of water toward the flames. Mom clutches me, strokes my hair, kisses my forehead. We're both shaking, crying. Sam puts his arms around us.

"Mom...Salty's at the spa, right?"

"Yes. Thank goodness for that."

There's an extremely loud booming sound. Firefighters rush out of the inn. One sinks to his knees, and another helps him up.

"Stand back everybody," a police officer shouts through a megaphone. "Across the street. Move it. Now!"

Flames pour out of the second-floor windows. All gone. There's an explosion. Sparks fly toward us. Mom, Sam, and I hurry across the street. Neighbors and curious tourists are huddled out front of No Mutts About It.

Two spa workers are standing on the steps. I run to them. "I want to see my dog," I shout. "The golden retriever. Salty Dog."

The workers look at each other and then back at me.

"Please," I sob. "I need to see my dog, *now*."

"I'm sorry," one of them says. "We were giving the dogs a final good-night fresh-air time in the run when the fireworks started. Salty bolted over the fence. We went out calling, looking for him, but we didn't want to alarm your family as it was late, and…."

"What? What do you mean? Where is he?" *What did you do!* I want to scream at them. I start running toward the house instead.

"Stop!" a firefighter shouts, arms around my waist, locking me in a grip.

"Please!" I struggle to break free. "My dog! My dog might be in there."

"I'm sorry, honey, but the captain called it. It's not safe for anyone to—"

"Willa," Sam reaches me, panting out of breath.

"Dad, please." I'm sobbing, gulping for air. "The workers said Salty bolted when the fireworks started, and they can't find him. We have to see if he's in there!"

"He got scared," Mom says. "He'll be back, don't worry."

"No! We…we have to get him!"

"Willa." Sam puts his palms on my face and locks eyes with me. "Listen to me. I know dogs, and no dog would stay in a burning house."

"Salty would," I sob. "Salty would do that to find me."

Chapter 6
No More Weddings

Failure is impossible.
—Susan B. Anthony

I wake up, and my first thought is, *What a horrible dream,* before reality comes crashing down on me. The Inn gone…Salty missing. I reek of smoke. I'm sleeping on the pullout couch in Nana's living room. She kissed my forehead gently before leaving for work this morning.

"Don't worry, sweetheart," she whispered. "Salty will turn up soon."

Oh, Salty, the tears come again.

I hear my parents talking in the kitchen.

"We're ruined, Sam. I need to cancel the Kardellian wedding—she's going to be devastated, and then I need to cancel every wedding on the books. There are deposits to be returned, vendor bills I can't pay. With the massive renovation loan, we were barely breaking even as it was. This bankrupts us."

"But, Stella. Once the insurance money…," Sam lowers his voice.

I get up and walk closer, standing in the hallway to listen.

"The insurance money will cover the loan. We can get out of debt and come out even, which is more than a lot of people would get in these circumstances."

"Stell, you can't be serious. This business is your baby."

"I'm empty, Sam. I've got nothing left to give. All the time and energy I put into growing my business, renovating the Inn, working my butt off twenty-four-seven. No. I can't do that all over again. I'm done."

"We all work hard," Sam says quietly.

"Yes, I know." Mom's voice rises. "But *I'm the wedding planner,* Sam. Brides aren't paying big bucks for cutesy charms in the cake."

I feel like my mom slapped me. The charms were my idea.

"Families are paying for *me,* Sam. Weddings by Havisham.

They're paying for the artistry, the expertise, the attention to every detail. They are paying for the notoriety of saying they had a 'Havisham wedding' like they brag about honeymoons in Fiji or Bora Bora."

"I know, sweetheart," Sam says. "And we are all so proud of you."

"I used to be proud of me, too, Sam." My mom's voice cracks. "But the joy is gone. I'm exhausted, physically, mentally, every way. I don't have the energy or desire to begin again. I need a break, time to figure out what I want, *what Stella wants*, to do next. I've shouldered the financial burden since Willa was a baby. I need you to step up now, Sam."

"What's that supposed to mean?" There's a hint of anger in Sam's voice.

"You need to find another job *now*. We need to at least make payroll. I'll give the staff notice today."

We're firing Darryl, Makita, Coby...everyone?

"I'll see which restaurants are hiring," Sam says.

"Restaurants lay off workers in August," Mom says. "You know that. What about Bramble Academy? Can you get your old job back?"

"That's Dr. Swaminathan's position now."

Mom knows that.

"It's late to be looking for a teaching job, Stell, but maybe I can pick up some adjunct courses at Cape Cod Community...I know the money's not good, but I'm being realistic. It's going to take time to find a good full-time job on Cape."

"Well, then maybe we should move."

What? No! I rush into the kitchen.

"Mom...We can't move!"

My mom looks at me sadly, takes a sip of coffee, sets the mug down, and touches the few bits of wedding paperwork she rescued from the fire.

I look at Sam, tears welling up.

"Good morning, Willa." He smiles and stretches out his arms, still smudged with soot from last night, and I gratefully go to him for a hug.

Sam won't let us move away.

"Good morning, Dad."

"I'm sorry if we woke you," he says. "I'll make you breakfast. Bacon and eggs?"

"Just toast for me." I sink down into a chair. Stella looks at me. I offer a sympathetic smile. I feel her pain, truly I do, but she's not thinking rationally here. "Please, Mom, let's talk about this. We can't leave Bramble. This is our home."

"Our home," she says quietly, "is destroyed."

"But *Bramble*," I yelp. "Cape Cod is our home. Everyone I love lives here."

"I'm sorry, Willa." Her voice rises. "We need to consider all of our options—the business is *ruined*."

"Yes, Mom, and that's horrible, but please don't ruin our life, too."

"Life costs money, Willa."

"We don't need a lot of money," I blurt out. "Why can't we live in one of the guest houses...they didn't burn...the Thoreau Lodge or the Hawthorne until the Inn is rebuilt?"

"And stare at the ravished remnants of the Inn," she says. "Breathing that awful stench, reliving last night again and again? No. I can't. You must understand that, Willa?"

I don't. I look to Sam for support.

He closes his eyes, then opens them, purses his lips and shakes his head slightly, as if to say, *Let it go for now, Willa.*

No. I can't. I won't. Old ugly feelings of disdain for my mom—for the cold-hearted woman she used to be—rise up inside me. Stella is the one who needs everything to be so fancy. Sam and I could be happy in a bunkhouse with a bookcase and a garden.

"It's not all about you, Mom. What about Sam and me? Don't our feelings count?"

A heavy veil of silence shrouds the room.

The toast pops up. Mom's cell phone beeps. She glances down and sighs loudly. "It was the wedding business that supported us, Willa." She rubs her temples. There are dark circles under her eyes. She probably didn't sleep at all last night.

"My wedding business—my work—everything I strived so hard to create is completely ruined...." Her voice catches. Sam puts his hand on her shoulder.

My mom sniffs, shakes her head, and sits up taller. "I don't have the energy...or the heart to start over. I need some time to think. Sam needs to be the sole breadwinner for this family for a while, and if that means our leaving Cape Cod, so be it."

"*So be it?*" I whisper in disbelief. My stomach churns in anger at the unfairness of it all, and at that moment, Stella seems responsible for everything that's gone wrong in our lives. "Why do you always have to run away, Mom?" The words come out as a scream. My body is shaking. I am sick to my stomach. This is the same thing she did for years, every time something went wrong. She reacted by packing our suitcases. "Why can't you stay? Why are you such a coward?"

"Willa!" Sam has never seen this side of me. Few people have.

"We are not running away, Willa," Stella responds, infuriatingly calm. "We are being responsible. That's what adults do. Sam has a much better chance of finding a good paying job off Cape than here and—"

"What about Salty?" I cut her off sharply, eyes shooting daggers at her. "Any news?"

"Not yet," Sam says.

"It seems you've got everything figured out, Mom. What's your plan for finding Salty?" I fold my arms across my chest; I don't want her to see how my hands are shaking.

My mom looks to Sam for an answer.

"I posted online, and I made up these flyers." Sam hands me one. It reads "Dog Missing," with a photo of Salty and contact info. "We can get these up all around town today. The staff at the pet spa are out searching at the Sivler's request. The police and fire departments are on the lookout, too, and I will call the shelters and veterinarian offices. The good thing is that Salty is wearing a collar. I've got my cell phone with me. I'm sure someone will call today."

"Oh, no," my mom says, with a worried look. "When I rounded up Salty for the spa yesterday, I took off his collar because I'd bought a new one with our green-and-gold Inn logo...."

"Mom," my heart stops beating. "Are you telling us Salty doesn't have a collar on?" She looks at the counter and nods. "So Salty has no identification." I start to cry.

"I'm sorry, Willa, I am," my mom says. "How could I have known...."

"Everybody in Bramble knows Salty Dog," Sam quickly reminds us.

"The tourists don't," I say. "What if he got hit by a car or someone decides to steal him? He's such a good dog. He's so friendly with everyone."

"Willa, I'm sure Salty will turn up today," Mom says in that same calm voice.

"You don't even like Salty!" I shout.

"Willa," Sam says, gently placing his hand on my shoulder. "Maybe Salty ran to the beach. You know how much he loves it there. I'll go with you if you want."

"That's a good idea, Dad. But I'll go alone. Nana has a bike in the garage. I just need to change..." And then I remember; I have no clothes.

"Your friend Chandler's mom called," my mom says. "She's bringing over clothes for all of us this morning."

"Who cares about clothes?" I shout at her. "I'm going now."

"Wait, Willa." Sam spreads peanut butter on the toast. "Take this."

"Thanks, Dad," I say.

"Good luck," my mom says. "Let me know if you find him!" she yells as I pedal down the driveway.

I don't respond. I can't speak to her right now. I can't even look at her.

Chapter 7
An Idea Sparks

This house sheltered us, we spoke, we loved within those walls. That was yesterday. To-day we pass on, we see it no more, and we are different, changed in some infinitesimal way. We can never be quite the same again.
—Daphne duMaurier, *Rebecca*

It's wrong that it's such a beautiful day. There should be storm clouds, thunder and lightning, torrential rain, sleet. I glare at the sunshine, the tourists. I want to say: *Do you know what's happening? My dog is lost! My mom is taking me away from my only home! And you're playing and singing and …vacationing!* It shouldn't be allowed.

I try to focus on Salty. *Please be there.* When I reach the ocean, heart pounding, I pray to hear his familiar bark over the cawing of gulls and crashing of waves. At the top of the stairs, I look down, right, left, then right again. People, boats, birds…no dogs.

I choke up, remembering the day I first met Salty here. He bounded toward me, knocking me backward on the sand he was so excited, slathering me with sloppy kisses, wet smelly fur. When our eyes met, he *smiled* at me. *Oh, Salty, where are you?*

Cupping my hands over my eyes to block that sun, I make my eyes be binoculars, scanning every inch of sand, water, jetties, banks of sea grass, as far as I can see. Salty and I love this beach. Our favorite time is right before dawn. He sits next to me on this top step here, my big furry pal, and we patiently wait for that diamond speck of sun to rise out of the sea. When it does, Salty barks and I laugh and hug him. *Happy new day, buddy.*

"*Salty.*" I clasp my hands over my heart. "Please, please, be okay."

Certain he's not at the beach, I bike into the center of Bramble, searching every yard, parking lot, store front and the alleys between them, headed toward Sweet Bramble Books.

The bells jangle as I open the door, and the sweet smell of fresh salt-water taffy wafts over me.

"Hello, sweetheart," Nana calls to me from the register where she's waiting on a customer. Her scruffy dog, Scamp, barks a welcome and runs to greet me. I bend down and let him lick my face with kisses. Muffles the cat meanders over and rubs against my leg.

Kristen and Amy, summer workers home from college, offer condolences about the fire.

"Willa, it there's anything I can do," Amy says, "just tell me."

"That goes without saying." Kristen hugs me. "You're our little sister. You know that."

"Please keep your eye out for Salty. And I do need to charge my phone."

"Here." Amy hurries behind the counter and comes back with a charger. "Take mine, Willa. Keep it. I've got another."

"Thanks, Amy."

"I'll look for Salty as soon as I get off work," Kristen says. "He'll turn up. You'll see."

"Thanks, Kristen." I manage a smile.

Nana finishes with her customer. She rushes over to hug me. The tears start again.

"Oh, sweetheart. Come, let's sit." We walk to the couch. Amy brings me a box of tissues.

"How are you holding up?" Nana asks, her face full of loving concern. "I still can't believe this happened. Thank God, no one was hurt. Any word on Salty?"

"No." I lean into her arms and cry. Nana pats my back.

I want to tell her that we may be moving, but then I'll start really sobbing, and that won't be good for business. I'll wait until she gets home later. *Home.*

"I'm praying extra prayers," Nana says. "Don't worry, sweetheart. Salty will turn up."

The door opens and Dr. Swaminathan enters. He helps Nana out part-time when school isn't in session. He reaches out to touch my arm in a formal, respectful manner. "Leslie and I are so sorry for your great loss, Willa. You must tell us how we can help."

Leslie (to me, forever *Mrs. Saperstone*) and Dr. Swaminathan are now married. It seems like a lifetime ago, but their wedding was just last weekend. I planned a small, yet elegant, evening affair in the library garden with hundreds of twinkle lights strung from the trees. I gave each guest a penny to offer the newlyweds before tossing it in the whale-spoutin' fountain. Mom said that was a lovely idea.

I am really good at planning weddings.

Wait. An idea sparks...a wonderfully exciting idea! *Stella Havisham may be finished planning weddings, but maybe the wedding planner's daughter can....*

"I've got to go!" I jump up.

Dr. S is not a hugger. Awkwardly, he reaches out his arms, leans in gently, his turban brushing against my head. "You are a strong girl. You will get through this."

When I get back to Nana's house, Chandler's mom, Mrs. Ryan, has already dropped off the clothes. There's a note from Chandler:

"We're so sorry about this, Willa. Answer your phone, okay? Emily, Trish, Greta, Lauren...all of us are looking for Salty. What else can we do to help?"

There's a message for me on the counter from Sam.

"Out looking for Salty, got some good leads. Then meeting with the insurance people. Joseph Kennelly called for you twice and some other boy who didn't leave a name. Be back soon. Love you, Sam (Dad)."

My mom is on Nana's computer, Skyping with a sobbing bride-to-be.

"Mom," I say quietly.

She looks at me for a second, shakes her head "no," and then refocuses on the bride.

"I realize how devastating this is for you, Janelle. And I am terribly sorry. Why don't you call me back later when you've had a chance to process—"

The screen goes blank. My mom groans. "I hate this!"

"Mom."

"Hi, Willa."

"Mom, can you look at me?" She looks up from the screen for a second. "I have a great idea."

"Just a second." She types something. "Your friend Tina reached out on Facebook. The Belles are in Saratoga, but she heard about the fire and feels awful. She said to tell you that she and Ruby are launching a social media campaign about Salty: tweeting and posting and pinning and—"

"That's nice, Mom, but listen. I thought of a way we can stay in Bramble. What if—"

"Oh, I have something to tell you, too! We have exciting news. Sam reached out to his network of friends from college and one of them responded already. Donna somebody-or-other is the dean of a college in upstate New York. One of her professors is going on unexpected leave, and she needs an English teacher immediately and would *love* to hire Sam. It's only a year guarantee, but the money is good, and it comes with a nice house all furnished and—"

"Mom, no, listen…"

"Sam and I Googled Troy—that's where the college is. It's about ten minutes from the capital city, Albany. Troy's an old river town, but it's undergoing quite an exciting renaissance—"

"Mom, *stop*! I am trying to tell you something *important*."

"I'm sorry, Willa, what?" Her phone beeps. She reads the message. "I need to take this, can we talk later?"

"Mom, wait, listen. We don't need to leave Bramble. I thought of a way we can stay."

Her phone beeps again. She looks up at the clock. "What are you talking about, Willa?"

"Mom, what if I planned the weddings? I'm good at it. You said so yourself. We don't need to have them at the Inn. There are lots of beautiful places on Cape—"

My mom looks baffled. She looks at Nana's computer screen. "I'm sorry, Willa. That's the Kardellian mom again. I really need to take this."

"Mom... *please pay attention to me*! You said I did a perfect job planning the S's wedding last weekend. That's the fourth successful one I've—"

"Yes, Willa." She types something. "But we need to make money here."

"I can make money. I—"

"Willa...," my mom sighs loudly. "You don't understand. We can't support a family on library courtyard soirees, however creative they are. I love your charms-in-the-wedding cakes notions, but cute ideas don't translate into a business plan. The real money, money we have built our life on, is with brides willing to pay the price for a 'Weddings by Havisham' work of art."

"So your weddings are masterpieces, and what, I'm just playing around?"

She scowls. "Willa, stop being so dramatic. I don't have time." Another beep. "I'm sorry. I have to take this."

"Mom, wait."

"Willa!" She flings her fists up in the air, exasperated. "Let this go." She types some keys and starts a new Skype session. She's back to being *the* Stella Havisham—Mom won't be around for the rest of the afternoon.

Chapter 8
The Labyrinth

Change is the law of life. And those who look only
to the past or present are certain to miss the future.
—John F. Kennedy

I take a shower and dress—running shorts and a Bramble Academy
soccer shirt. Chandler and I are about the same size; the clothes fit well.
My pink Chucks are black with soot.

Sam must still be meeting with the insurance people at the Inn.
I will bike there and talk to him. Maybe if we combine forces, we can
change Mom's mind. I can't imagine leaving Bramble. I shake my head.
I can't even handle the thought of going somewhere else. I can't believe
she's being so…Stella! *And* she *calls* me *dramatic.*

A block away from our street, I smell the smoke, the stench
growing stronger and stronger as I get closer. At the edge of our property,
I reach out and run my hand along the long row of tall green shrubs
standing sentinel. *You didn't guard us very well last night,* I tell them as I
pass by.

I gulp when I see the Bramble Board. One of my jobs is (was?
No) to post a daily inspirational message. Writers always mention it in the
magazine articles about us.

Things like:

Go confidently in the direction of your dreams.

— Henry David Thoreau

That was the first quote I saw Sam putting up back when Mom
and I first moved to Bramble, back when I called him "the poet," back
when Sam was just my really handsome, kind, smart English teacher, back
before I ever imagined he would be the father I'd always wished for, in a
hometown I'd always dreamed of. Now, all my dreams have burst like tiny
bubbles in one awful night.

Resting Nana's bike against the gate, I stare at the still-smoldering charred shell of our home. I have so many memories here: our new life, finally finding a place I can belong. This is where Will, my half-brother, found me and where we became a family. I think of all the silly times I had with our staff in the kitchen, the hours spent reading and journaling in my bedroom. Tears well up and a sob escapes. I sit on the ground and wrap my arms around my knees.

Police officers and firefighters are still milling about. One waves at me, and the other nods and smiles a sad smile. Strangers, perhaps from the insurance company or newspaper, are taking photographs and jotting notes.

"Here, honey," a woman says, handing me a packet of tissues. "Can I get you some water or something?"

"No, thank you." I blow my nose and try to get a grip. I know where Sam is.

Trying to avoid mounds of debris, I make a wide loop around to the backyard. There's the beautiful labyrinth Sam so skillfully and lovingly crafted. And there he is, in the middle, sitting on the stone bench, with his eyes closed.

I enter and walk the familiar path, bordered on both sides by perennial flowers—Shasta daisies, black-eyed Susans, purple cone flowers, tall red Bee Balm—circling in toward the heart of the circle, then out again…in, then out, until I reach the center.

There is a peaceful expression on Sam's face. "Dad?" I speak softly.

He opens his eyes and smiles. I wish everyone in the world could have someone who smiles at you like that, letting you know, no matter what, everything will be okay.

"Come, sit." He pats the spot beside him.

We tell each other what we've done to find Salty. "What's the news here?" I ask.

"The investigators say the fire started in the basement, most likely electrical in origin, then rapidly ran up the walls. Old buildings like this, the way they're constructed, they go quickly."

I reach out to clasp Sam's hand and squeeze it. "Listen." I tell him about my idea to take over the wedding planning business. "Of course, Mom doesn't believe I can do it, but maybe we can talk some sense into her and then we won't have to leave Bramble."

Sam listens, eyes-to-eyes, until I'm finished, not interrupting or looking away even once. He thinks about what I've said. He puts his arm around my shoulder. "You're wonderful, Willa."

A greenish-gold hummingbird alights on a pink honeysuckle bush, tiny wings flickering, then flits away fast.

"When my grandmother willed this house to me," Sam says, looking back at what was once the old Gracemore Estate, "I was surprised and overwhelmed. It had been vacant for years. I had no idea how to restore it. I was an English teacher, an aspiring writer. I never dreamed it could become such a fine place. That was all your mom's vision, Willa, right from the very start."

I nod. "I remember the first time you invited us here, for a barbecue, and gave us a tour. All the furniture was covered in sheets, thick dusty drapes, cobwebs everywhere. You showed us your writing studio upstairs with the old captain's desk and your books. When you said you were *writing a book*, I was so excited to ask you about it, but Mom was already counting bedrooms, calculating rates, and saying what a 'fortune' you could make."

Sam laughs. "Your mom scared me to death that night. She was stunning and smart, quite spectacular. So far out of my league. What would she ever see in me?"

"Are you kidding, Dad? You're a great catch."

"A catch?" Sam laughs. "What am I, a fish?"

"It's not fair that she's making us leave Cape Cod."

"Willa," Sam says quietly, staring into my eyes. "Your mom works hard. She appreciates a certain lifestyle. She likes nice things, yes, but she *loves* you and me."

"She's making us leave Bramble! This is our home."

"Home is where the people you love are. We can make any place

45

home."

"But wouldn't you miss Bramble?" My voice is squeaking.

"Of course, sweetheart. But your mom has more than carried the lion's share of the financial burden on this family. It's my turn."

"But you can get a chef job at another inn."

"The season's ending, Willa. Restaurants are laying off, not hiring. And, honestly, as much as I love cooking, I miss the classroom more."

I knew it. "You *are* a great teacher."

"Thank you, Willa. I appreciate that."

I look at the bountiful flowers, the birds, the tranquil pond in the distance. I think of how peaceful Sam's face looked when I got here, *happy about the idea of teaching again.* Sam deserves a chance to follow his dreams.

But what about my dreams? What about my happiness?

We sit there silently side by side. I take a deep breath in and let it out, focusing on the breathing as Sam taught me, feeling calmer by the moment.

It's only for a year. By then Stella will have come to her senses, and we can come home. "Mom told me about the offer you got this morning. What's the name of the school?"

"Russell Sage College. It's in Troy, in Upstate New York. Donna Heald, the dean, is a former classmate and good friend. I have the upmost respect for her. I'd be teaching an American Lit class, English Lit, poetry, and public speaking—courses I love, that I miss. This is a temporary appointment, but Donna says there a there's a good chance..."

A good chance? A good chance we'll stay there for good? Oh, no.

"There's a book-making business in Troy that interests me, also," Sam says. "As soon as we get settled in Troy"—there's excitement in his voice—, "I'm going to carve out one hour every day to write. I know my best poems will come back to me."

Settled in Troy. So this is really happening.

Sam has done so much for me and Mom. "When?"

"When, what?"

"When do we have to go?

Sam touches my arm, then puts his hands on my shoulders and locks eyes with mine.

"I know this is hard for you, Willa, truly I do. And if there were a way I could think of to stay here financially..."

"But, Dad," the words blurt out, "I really could run a wedding business."

"And you would be great at that," he says with conviction. "You've already proven so. But right now you're starting your sophomore year in high school."

High school. What high school? I can't even get the words out.

"Your job, Willa, is to get a good education. Our job is to support that."

I burst into tears. Sam hugs me. I blow my nose, wipe my face.

"We'll come home, though, when this teaching job is over, right? I'm willing to give that Troy place a chance, but I can't bear to lose Bramble forever."

"We'll see, Willa. So much depends on the insurance company settlement, and what your mom decides career-wise, and, who knows, we might find we like Troy."

I doubt that. No place compares to Bramble.

"Change can be good, Willa. Life surprises us."

I hate surprises.

We sit quietly, lost in our thoughts.

"Okay." I finally stand up, brushing ash and flower petals off my shorts. "Let's go find Salty."

"You first," Sam says.

I start walking back out of the labyrinth, circling in, then out, closer, then farther away, glad that I'm in front of Sam, so he can't see the tears streaming down my cheeks.

When we reach the statue of the girl reading a book, Sam puts his arm around my shoulder. "Shall we bring her with us to Troy? The house has a nice yard."

"No. She belongs here in Bramble."

Like me.

Chapter 9
The Real World

You've got a light that always guides you
You speak of hope and change as something good...
—Sarah McLachlan, "In Your Shoes"

We search around town for Salty for hours. I put air in the tires of Nana's bike, then head to Mum's house. I always feel better after talking to Mum.

She and Riley are sitting on the front porch. Their faces light up when they see me.

"How are you, sugar?" Riley kisses me on the cheek. "We're so sorry about the fire."

"Hanging in there," I say. "How about you?"

"I'm sitting here with my better three-quarters, looking at a field of sunflowers." He winks at Mum. "Life doesn't get much sweeter than that."

I laugh. Riley always makes me laugh.

"Come here, baby," Mum pulls me in for a hug. She's lost weight, probably those awful chemotherapy treatments. I want desperately to tell her what's happening, but she has her own burden to deal with.

"How are you feeling, Mum?"

"Fine." She smiles, holding up her ample breasts and bouncing them. "These girls have their gloves on. We're fighting back hard."

"That's great," I muster a smile.

"That's right," Riley says, his face shining with love for his wife.

"I've got a good doctor down here," Mum says, "and a *great* doctor up there." She points to the sky. "Nothing we can't beat."

"You'll be fine." My eyes well up. I always come to Mum for support, but leaving the Cape is nothing compared to cancer. I swipe the tears quickly and smile. "Your garden looks great, Mum."

"Come on, honey. You can help me." She hands me a basket. I follow her.

Two scarecrows guard the sunflowers, bright-yellow petal hair, round brown faces.

"Look at this silly family," Mum says, pointing.

A fat gray squirrel pulls a sunflower down to the ground and scarfs up seeds at a frantic pace, black shell-bits flying everywhere. Other squirrels attempt similar maneuvers.

"They think it's Thanksgiving," Mum jokes. "Stealing all of our good sunflower seeds." She shakes her head. "Riley stuck our Halloween scarecrows out thinking that might keep the bandits away. The scarecrows may be scaring crows, but they sure aren't worrying the squirrels. Riley says the squirrels probably think they are waiters in a restaurant."

Mum and I laugh. It feels good to laugh. "I love sunflowers."

"Me, too. Sunflowers are *our flowers.*"

Mum and Riley are together because of me. They had been teenage sweethearts then separated for decades. I encouraged Mum to track him down and write him a letter. One day Riley showed up handsome in a suit with a bouquet of flowers, walked straight up the aisle at BUC to Mum and said, "Will you marry me?" It was the most romantic thing I have ever witnessed in my entire life. Mum asked me to be her maid of honor; I was so proud. They moved into this house and planted a garden, rows and rows of sunny sunflowers, and every one made me smile.

Last year, when Mum and Riley announced they were leaving Bramble for a congregation closer to family in South Carolina, I bought a huge bunch of sunflowers at Delilah's Florist in town and gave them to her as a parting gift. As they drove away, Mum threw a flower out the window and said she'd keep tossing them all the way to her new home so that the seeds would sprout and all I'd have to do would be to "follow the sunny road" to find her.

Now I'm the one who is leaving.

The short walk to the vegetable section has left Mum out of breath. She points. "Pull that head of lettuce there, girl, and a cuke and some tomatoes. Whatever your family likes. I want to make you a nice salad to take home."

"That reminds me. Thank you for the pie you sent this morning, Mum. What kind is it?"

"Peach. Is there any other?"

Mum and I sit on the porch. Riley brings us sweet tea and a plate of sugar cookies. "I'll leave you two girls to talk," he says.

I sip the tea, nibble on a cookie, forcing myself not to dump all of my pain on Mum.

"Spill it, sister," Mum says as if reading my mind.

Gratefully, I blurt out all about Salty and how selfish Stella is being and how we're leaving Bramble for some stupid place called Troy and what a jerk JFK is being and….

Mum listens and nods and waits 'til I'm done. She smiles and pats my arm.

"Why do things have to change, Mum?"

"That's life, baby. Everything is always changing. But *you*…." She points to me. "The Willa I know…the girl who loves so much and hopes for the best and is always finding ways to help others…, that won't change…that's you. Always Willa. That's the constant you count on. That, and knowing that all the people who love you, even though they may be miles away or in heaven already…all the people you love are right there in your heart, believing in you, cheering you on, ready to catch you if you fall."

Mum taps her heart then reaches over to tap mine. "Right there, baby, always. No distance ever changes that."

"Hey, Mama," Riley calls out the window, "should I start peeling the shrimp for dinner?"

"Yes, babe, thanks. Be sure to devein them, too. You know how to do that, right?"

"Willa," Riley calls to me. "Will you please tell my queen that, of course, I know how to scoop the poop out of shrimp. I was born at night, but it wasn't last night."

Mum and I laugh. My phone beeps. Sam has a "good lead on

Salty." *Thank God!*

"Gotta go, Mum."

"Okay, little sister. Now listen to me. We are not going to say goodbye, just 'til soon with balloons' or something like that."

I laugh, then start to cry.

"Go ahead," Mum says. "It is sad. Cry your eyes out leaving Bramble, crossing over that Bourne Bridge, cry all the way to New York if you have to...*but*...when you see that 'Welcome to Troy' sign, this is what you are going to do. Help your Mom and Sam unpack, set up your new bedroom, call all your friends here to let us know you've arrived, and then,"—Mum points to my feet— "lace up those snazzy pink sneakers of yours and start enjoying Troy. Check out your new school, meet the neighbors, explore the town. Walk those city streets like you walk the beach here, and I know, I know because I know *you* and that big beautiful heart of yours...that you will meet wonderful people and make new friends and find your next way to pay your rent."

There's a crashing sound in the kitchen and Riley says a word we won't repeat. Mum huffs. "What mess is that man making in my kitchen now?" She shakes her head. We laugh.

"Focus on serving others, Willa, and you won't be focusing on your own pain."

"Get out of myself and get busy helping others, that's what you preach, Mum."

She points down. "And stick those sneaks in the washer before you travel. The soot should come right out."

"I'll try to put my best feats forward. F, e, e, t, s...sneakers...and f, e, **A**, t, s...service."

Mum laughs. "That's my girl. Now let me quick make that salad for you."

"Oh no, Mum, I can do that at home. You better check on Riley."

"Okay, then. Take the basket." Mum chuckles. "Put your best feats forward. I like that. Mind if I use that in my sermon on Sunday?"

"Go right ahead. I'd be honored. And thanks for letting me talk,

Mum."

"That's what friends are for, baby. That's what friends are for."

I start down the steps.

"Wait, Willa," Mum says. She reaches into a pail and hands me a pair of scissors. "Go clip a bouquet of sunflowers to take back to your grandmother's."

Riley pops his head out of the window. "Watch out for those crazy squirrels, though."

*****

Biking back to Nana's, I feel lighter, more hopeful. I bet Salty will tackle me as soon as I open the door, barking all happy to see me, and I'll hug that golden fur coat and let him slobber my face with kisses. "I love you, love you," and he'll bark "I love you, I love you more."

When I see the expression on Sam's face, it is clear there is nothing to celebrate.

"I'm sorry, Willa. It wasn't Salty."

Bursting into tears, I slam the sunflowers and vegetables on the counter, run to Nana's bedroom, slam the door, and collapse on her bed.

Hours later, I get up and go to the kitchen for some water. I stop and listen as Nana is talking to my mom in a very stern voice.

"I don't like what I'm reading about crime in Troy."

"Troy's a city, Mom. All cities have issues."

"I don't want you taking my granddaughter somewhere that's not safe."

"I would never put Willa in danger," Mom snaps. "You can't keep her cloistered on Cape Cod forever. Bramble is not the real world."

It's my world, though.

Chapter 10
Rooting for the Underdog

*Sometimes we are lucky enough to know that our
lives have been changed, to discard the old, embrace the
new, and run headlong down an immutable course.*
—Jacques Cousteau

Saturday is another day of searching, but no Salty. Our veterinarian
assured us that Salty would not have stayed in a burning building. It's
possible he was traumatized by the incident, got disoriented, and wasn't
able to find his way back. JFK's father, editor of *The Cape Cod Times,* was
good about printing a story and "lost dog" notices in the paper. There are
posters up all over town, and the "Find Salty" Facebook page that Tina
started has 320 "likes." *Oh Salty, hurry home. We're leaving Bramble on
Friday.*

I scroll through messages from friends, from JFK, from Jessie.
I talk with my brother, Will. He wishes he could zip right back over the
pond right now to be with me, but he can't.

Mariel calls that night and talking to her helps me feel a bit
better. She's having a great time in New York. I tell her how happy I am
for her, and she mentions that Troy isn't all that far from New York City.
"Maybe three hours. You could take the train next school break; I've been
dying to show you everything in New York!" I tell her I'll think about it,
but even that doesn't change my attitude towards Troy. It will always be
the city that took me away from my home.

Sam is reading the packet of materials his friend from Sage sent
him, studying the faculty handbook, reviewing the curricula for his
courses, brushing up on the first books his students will be reading. He
keeps checking on me every few hours, trying to get me to eat something.

Mom is glued to Nana's computer, making her way through her
brides and vendors lists, severing one contract after another. They all
have to be moved to nearby inns and hotels, new cooks and bakers need

55

to be called, DJs and bands have to be kept in the loop. Stella probably made over a hundred calls, but by the end of the day, instead of looking exhausted, she actually looks refreshed. She asks Nana and me if we want to go shopping for clothes.

I decline. I ignore the hurt on her face as she leaves the house with Nana.

Sam's watching a sports show in the living room. He calls out, "Willa, come here! The Travers Stakes race is on TV."

"Tina and her family are there," I say, sinking down next to him on the couch. Two sports announcers are talking excitedly about Triple Crown Winner American Pharaoh.

"Mr. Belle has a horse in the race. Keen Ice. Tina says he's a real long shot. I gave her two dollars to bet on him to win."

"Rooting for the underdog," Sam says. "I like that."

During a commercial, Sam gets us some sandwiches, soda, and chips. We watch as the horses are led out of the paddock. "There's your horse," Sam says. "He's a beauty."

The jockey is wearing green and gold. "Green and gold," I say sadly.

"I know," Sam squeezes my hand.

Green and gold were our colors at the Inn. All the tablecloths and towels....

"Here we go," Sam says as the last horse moves into the starting gate.

"And they're off," the announcer shouts.

American Pharaoh leads the pack as predicted, but Keen Ice starts off strong. I keep my eyes peeled on him. "Come on, buddy, come on."

"Wow," Sam says. "Look at him go."

Thousands of people are screaming for Pharaoh, but I'm rooting for the underdog. He's in third, now second and gaining ground.

"You can do it. You can do it. Come on, Keen Ice, come on," I yell.

"And Keen Ice wins the race!" the announcer shouts.

I jump up cheering. My phone beeps. It's Tina. "Willa, we won!" She posts pictures of her and Ruby wearing chic summer dresses and fancy race-track hats. Mr. Belle looks elated. I hope Tina told him that I believed his horse could win.

"On a two-dollar wager, you just won thirty-four dollars," Sam says. "You've got good horse sense, Daughter."

*****

Mom and Nana return with shopping bags. "Great end of summer sales," Mom says in a bubbly voice. "Let's go out tonight, babe," she says to Sam. "Something fun. A date night." She changes into a new outfit, fixes her hair and makeup.

"How can she be so happy?" I ask Nana after they leave.

"Not happy so much as relieved, honey. She's been under tremendous stress this year."

"Really? Why didn't she ever say anything to me?"

"I don't think she had a choice," Nana says. "She knew she had to keep going to pay off that loan. And, besides, parents don't like to burden their children with—"

"Burden me? Leaving Bramble is the burden, Nana."

"I know, sweetheart. I bet this is only temporary, though. Come on, let's order pizza with all the toppings and find a good movie to watch. A comedy. Something really silly."

The movie is funny, but there's a dog in it. The dog is a mutt who doesn't look anything at all like Salty, but that doesn't matter to me.

"Salty will come home, Willa. I'm sure of it."

*****

On Sunday morning, my mom is sitting at the kitchen table, sipping coffee, reading. She's wearing a pretty blue top and a patterned hair band that sets off her stunning black hair.

"Good morning, Willa." She smiles brightly. "I printed out all of this information on Troy for us to look at." She pulls out a chair. "Come here. I'll show you."

"No thanks." I pour water, set the kettle on the stove, turn on the burner and leave.

When the whistle blows, she calls, "I've got it, Willa. Do you want regular or herbal?"

"I'll get it myself." I grab the kettle off the burner, quickly pouring the steaming water into one of Nana's oversized mugs. I dunk my tea bag silently as Stella continues to talk.

"Can I at least show you some pictures of Troy," she says, holding up one of the sheets. "Look at these historic buildings. The downtown is really nice—"

"No, thanks."

"There's a park with two lakes right by our house."

Our house? I could scream. I dunk the tea bag with a vengeance, squeeze it dry, then toss it in the trash.

"You should start getting ready for church, Willa."

"I'm not going."

"Why?"

I don't respond. *I can't bear to sit next to you for an hour.*

*****

Chandler calls. "Mum's sermon was about putting your best feats forward in life. She mentioned you and your pink sneakers, Willa."

"That's nice."

Tina texts me. She's home from Saratoga and feels so bad about the fire and Salty, and wishes she could come over and give me a big hug right this minute, but she needs to prepare for her launch party tonight. "You're coming, right?"

"Sure. I'll be there."

I don't go.

We're going to visit Troy tomorrow. "Just for the day, over in the morning, back at night," my mom says. "To check out the house, and a school for you."

"I have a meeting with my friend, the dean at Sage," Sam adds. "It's a really nice campus, in the heart of the city, right across from the Troy Public Library. I think you'll like it."

The only library I like is *my library*, the Bramble Library.

The next morning, I feign a stomach bug and convince them to go without me.

"I'll stay home with Willa today," Nana says.

We watch television—game shows and sitcoms; Nana changes channels whenever a dog appears.

*****

In bed, I think about how Keen Ice won the race despite the odds. The crowd was rooting for the champion. I rooted for the underdog.

I'm rooting for you Salty. Hurry, hurry home.

Chapter 11
A Movie Called *Goodbye*

*I read and walked for miles at night along the
beach, writing bad blank verse and searching endlessly for
someone wonderful who would step out of the darkness
and change my life. It never crossed my mind that that
person could be me.*

—Anna Quindlen

The next day, on the kitchen counter, there's a brochure, student
handbook, curriculum guide, and fall sports schedule for Troy High
School, and some dates and notes about classes—required and electives.
There's a note from my mom:

> *Good morning, Willa. Hope you're feeling better. The
> faculty house is adorable, and Troy High seems like a great
> school. Take a look at this stuff and let me know what you
> think.*

I don't read any of it.

Later, when Mom asks, I nod and say, "Yeah, I saw it."

As leaving day approaches, Sam and Mom are busy tying up loose
ends. There are meetings with the fire chief, the insurance company, the
bank. Stella comes back from each of these meetings looking more and
more rejuvenated, and even Sam has a bit of a spring in his step. It seems
like I'm the only one not looking forward to the big move.

I keep checking with the pet spa, the Humane Society, all the
veterinarians in town, the local police, and social media, hoping for any
clue about Salty. "We can't leave Bramble without him," I insist.

Mom and Sam look at each other. Mom looks down. Sam purses
his lips and tries to look hopeful. "The semester has already started, Willa.
I need to get to Troy."

"And you need to start school," Mom says, looking up from the
newspaper she's been reading. "Huh," she says, pointedly trying to get me

61

to ask what she's reading. When I don't take the bait, she keeps reading. "The US government is finally going to put a woman on US currency. They're talking about Elizabeth Cady Stanton or Susan B. Anthony, maybe even together, on the new ten-dollar bills."

I know Susan B. Anthony, but the other name sounds vaguely familiar. I don't ask who they are. Figures my mom would be all excited about a story about money.

"Willa and I were talking about the Equal Rights Amendment recently." Sam looks at me.

"It doesn't mean anything," I state bluntly as I stalk out of the room. I go back to Nana's room and shut the door.

I lay on Nana's bed for hours, staring at the ceiling. She brings me books, but none of them hold my interest. She brings me candy. I don't eat it.

Normally when I'm feeling down, I write. I write myself through the tough times, pouring out my pain on the page until I feel better again. This time, I have no heart to write, no spark, no desire at all. I can't read. I can't write. I am numb.

"Here, try this one," Nana says, handing me a book with a bright turquoise cover entitled *Wonder*. I read the flap copy. It's about a boy named Auggie who has grotesque facial deformities and is about to start middle school. Middle school is hard enough for anybody—I can't imagine how difficult it would be if people thought you looked like a monster.

I start reading and, thankfully, get lost in the story. I read all day until the end. I re-read the line I highlighted on page 231:

"I think there should be a rule that everyone in the world should get a standing ovation at least once in their lives."

I got applause like that once, when I made my plea to save the Bramble Library. I still remember how nervous I was going in front of the City Council, and how proud I was when they stood up and applauded. Auggie would understand that it's not about the attention or the praise. It's more about the fact that you did something good, something that makes the world somehow better, and the standing ovation is just a way of saying that they're right there with you. *I agree, Auggie,* I think before I drift off to sleep. *Everyone should get that at least once.*

*****

The days pass by in slow motion as if I'm dreaming or in a vacuum, submerged under water, inside a plastic bubble, watching a movie called *Goodbye*, and not really hearing or talking or moving or feeling, observing this girl named Willa who could be my identical twin. It's a very engaging movie, so sad that I would normally be crying, but I watch from the other side of the screen, safely removed from really feeling that girl Willa's pain.

I cannot shake the feeling that the movie will end any second now. And then I'll get to walk out of the theater and go back to my life. But no; it keeps going on and on. All I can do is watch.

I watch Willa say goodbye to her friends. Tina and Ruby throw her a surprise sleepover party, and all the girls from school come: Chandler, Greta, Carli, Kelsie, Shefali, Caroline, Lauren, Lexy, Emily, Allison, and Trish. They bring her presents: clothes and jewelry, perfume and music. Tina tells Willa to keep an eye out for Sawyer Fredericks, the cute boy who won *The Voice*. His family has a farm not too far from Troy.

"He started out playing guitar and singing on corners in Saratoga where I was this week," Ruby gushes to the other girls.

"He's an old soul like you," Tina says. Her eyes fill with tears, and she hugs Willa tight. "I can't believe I'm losing you after everything!"

I watch Willa say goodbye to the two boys who like her, JFK and Jessie.

"I'm sorry for hurting you," JFK says.

"Let me know what the music scene is like in Troy," Jessie says. She hugs them both.

I watch Willa say goodbye to all these nice people at Bramble United Community, especially the minister, Sulamina Mum and her husband, Riley.

I watch Willa say goodbye to the Bramble librarians, Mrs. Saperstone and Ms. Toomajian, her favorite reading chair and the whale-spoutin' fountain in the courtyard where Mrs. S suggests she toss a coin and make a wish, but Willa doesn't.

I watch her say goodbye to her teachers at Bramble Academy. The one named Dr. Swaminathan has tears in his eyes.

I watch her say goodbye to Darryl, Makita, Mae-Alice, and Coby, the staff of the now-destroyed Bramblebriar Inn, which used to be her home.

I watch her say goodbye to Scamp and Muffles and the employees at Sweet Bramble Books.

"Don't worry, Willa," everyone says.

"We'll find Salty."

"Thanksgiving will be here before you know it."

"A year goes by fast."

"You'll be back."

"We love you!"

She can only give them a weak smile.

*****

On our final day, I bike to the Inn to say goodbye. I explain to the statue why she has to stay in Bramble, and I take one last walk through the labyrinth. I can't cry; I can barely even breathe. The air still smells a bit like smoke, but that's not it. I spend hours just sitting on the charred grass, staring at what's left of our home.

Later I bike down Main Street, soaking it all in. Nothing has changed in Bramble over the last few weeks, but to me, everything looks completely different. I don't stop in anywhere; I couldn't handle seeing anyone today.

Then I head to the beach for one last walk. *Come on Salty*, I think as I stumble over some seaweed. *This is your last chance buddy*. I spot an orange jingle shell, my favorite, but I don't pick it up. I see a piece of green sea glass and then, farther, a blue one, a mermaid's tear. I leave them for another to find.

I picture the jar of jingle shells and beach glass I used to have on the window ledge of my bedroom at home. My rainbow jar. How many times it made me smile. So many treasures I collected on this beach. Salty was the best of all. I close my eyes desperately hoping to hear his bark. *Please Salty, hurry. It's almost time for us to leave.*

Chapter 12
The Bourne Bridge

*Forget conventionalism; forget what the world
thinks of you stepping out of your place; think your best
thoughts, speak your best words, work your best works,
looking to your own conscience for approval.*
—Susan B. Anthony

As we pull out of Nana's driveway, she waves and blows kisses, and I wave
back until I can't see her anymore. Through blurry eyes, I keep staring out
the back window, praying that maybe Salty will appear. He'll see us and
come running like a race horse, valiantly, panting, and out of breath 'til he
reaches us, Salty the Super Dog.

But there's no Salty, just cars and trucks and miles and miles, each
one separating me further from all that I love. We are nearing the Bourne
Bridge. Sam is driving, Mom next to him. I don't think she even shed a
tear. I am in the backseat without my dog beside me, wearing new gray
sweats and a hoodie from Nana, my scuffed but still pretty pink Chucks—
the only thing to make me smile.

I'm surrounded by all my earthly possessions…my good-luck
gifts.

Tina and Ruby gave me a whole fall wardrobe—"The 70's stuff is
in," Tina said, "bell-bottoms, loose tops, suede and fringe, faux fur vests,
everything denim."—and five copies of *The Smart Girl's Guide to the Best
Beaches on Cape Cod*. "Give these to girls at your new school," Ruby said.
"This will be your ticket in."

My other friends gave me clothes, too; a basket of lotions and
perfumes from Victoria's Secret; scented candles, jewelry, makeup, and
music. Chandler came to my farewell sleepover, and I remembered what
I had thought about the fire having "silver linings." *Figures, I'd move to
another state just as I get a chance to reconnect with an old friend.*

Chandler made me a "girls rule" playlist. "My aunt went to a famous high school for girls in Troy called Emma Willard," she told everyone proudly. She brought up pictures on her phone to show us.

"Wow," Lauren said. "Is that where you're going? It even looks nicer than Bramble Academy."

"No. Public school for me."

"You're better off, Willa," Ruby said. "No uniforms."

"And who wants to go to a school without boys?" Tina said.

*****

I keep looking through my goodbye gifts. There's a Sweet Bramble Books box filled with thirty little bags of candy from Nana—one bag a day for a month—saltwater taffy, gummy fish, cherry cordials, all my favorites. And there's a card promising to send more in October and "then you'll be home for Thanksgiving!!" There's another Sweet Bramble Books box full of books selected by the S's—there must be two dozen here—a few favorites like *Anne of Green Gables*, another copy of *I Am Malala,* and other titles they thought I would enjoy.

There's a pouch of sunflower seeds from Mum's garden to "plant when you get there" and ten crisp ten-dollar bills from her and Riley —a "rainy-day fund for something fun." I look at the bills and remember the article Mom mentioned the other day. Maybe in a year or so I can turn these in for newly minted Elizabeth Cady Stanton or Susan B. Anthony bills.

We're heading toward the Bourne Bridge now. I start to cry, watching as we cross the Bourne Bridge in the "wrong" direction, the away-from-Cape-Cod direction, away from Salty-and-the-people-I-love direction, away from my ocean and my beach and Bramble....Our car crests the top, and I look down, diamond-lights sparkling on the waves. I've cried so much in these past few weeks that I could have formed a new ocean by now.

Tina Googled Troy, New York, and it's "the home of Uncle Sam." Big deal. So what. A cartoon character.

Our Sam is listening to National Public Radio. Mom has her ear buds in, probably listening to the latest *NY Times* bestseller on how to ruin your teenage daughter's life. I open the window, breathing in that last bit of warm ocean air.

My heart clenches remembering the joy and hope I felt on that magical day when Mom and I crossed this bridge in the *right* direction, to the perfect small town: Bramble. I'd never really had a home before.

When I was young, and Mom and I lived in all those different cities—Washington… Baltimore…Philadelphia…Newark…Hartford… Providence—she would always take me to Cape Cod to visit Nana in the summer. I'd get so excited seeing that big blue Welcome to Cape Cod sign, I'd stick my head out the window and wave. When vacation ended, I'd wave again, this time saying goodbye. When I found out we were moving here for good, that Bramble would be our home, I thought I'd burst with happiness. I think of that little girl Mikaela on the beach, "You live on Cape Cod? You're so lucky."

Yes, I was.

I will never say goodbye to Bramble, ever. I'll be back for Thanksgiving, then Christmas, then winter break, and spring break. And then Sam's teaching gig will be over, and Mom will have come to her senses, and we'll be back here next summer for good. It's only one school year, that's all. Maybe Sam can get a post at a Boston-area college and commute. It's only an hour off the Cape. And even though she's tired and sick of weddings right now, I know my mom will start itching to run a business again: it's in her MBA blood. By that time, the insurance settlement money should be in, and we'll be able to rebuild.

I think about JFK. I was heartbroken by our breakup, but then after the fire and losing my house and having to move and Salty still missing…I have way more important things to focus on. What will Troy be like? The people? The house? My new school?

My last gift from Bramble is from Dr. Swammy and Mrs. Saperstone. They dropped off a box of books at Nana's last night, with a note that says:

"We couldn't resist. Here are some more new friends for your new home."

I held off opening the box of books and made sure to put it next to me in the car. I carefully open the top. There's one by David Almond, one of my favorite authors, and another called *Speak* by Laurie Halse Anderson.

I can't help but think of all of the books in the personal library in my bedroom…all of those in the Inn library downstairs. I think about all of my journals. I haven't started a new one yet. I still don't feel like writing. There are not words for all the things I'm feeling right now.

Will I ever feel like writing again?

Troy

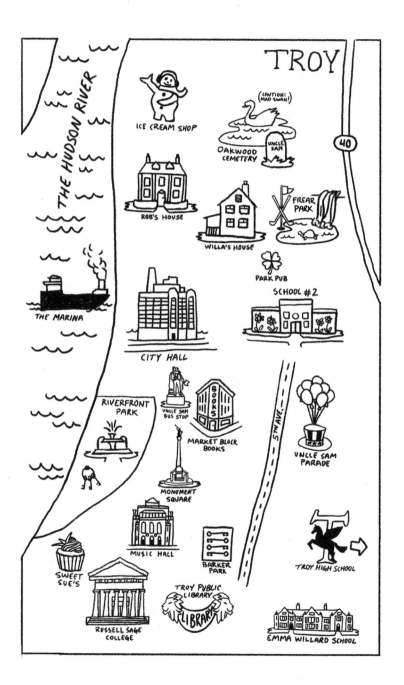

Chapter 13
Welcome to Troy, New York

Never believe that a few caring people can't
change the world. For indeed, that's all who ever have.
—Margaret Mead

Stomach growling, I open the lunch box from our friends at the
Moonakis Café. Mom and I used to always stop there on our way out of
town, and Nana insisted we all go there this morning. It's our favorite spot
for breakfast, but I couldn't eat a thing. The manager and her daughter
hugged us. The owner took pictures and tried to make me smile. "Don't
worry, Willa," he said. "You'll be back."

I will be.

I better be.

I take a bite of the grilled chicken with pesto sandwich, pop a
grape in my mouth, and stare out the window. Unable to focus on any of
the scenery, I untie the ribbon from one of the little bags of candy Nana
gave me. I choose a lemon-lime taffy, smiling sadly at the tag, "Be Happy,
Eat Taffy." The tags were my idea. Something that would make Sweet
Bramble Books taffy stand out from every other store on the Cape. Nana
says it's the reason she finally won "best candy shop on the Upper Cape"
in the *Cape Cod Life* magazine competition.

The sugar lifts my spirits the teeniest bit. I pull out my phone
and Google "Troy, New York." The official website for the city of Troy is
boring, but a lot of official things are. I try not to hold it against them. I
read the headlines from the local papers. The Troy mayoral primary is
too close to call. The governor of New York is pushing for a fifteen-dollar
minimum wage throughout the state. Sunday is the Uncle Sam Parade. *An
Uncle Sam Parade? Really?* That seems excessive.

An article in the newspaper catches my eye. A young couple
from Brooklyn, Vic Christopher and Heather Lavine, fell in love with
Troy, moved there, and renovated two old buildings into apartments, a

chic wine bar, and an upscale restaurant, with more plans on the way. The article has a quote from Vic: "…buildings that are affordable…that's what inspires creativity. People need space to do cool stuff. Troy is diverse, sometimes gritty…endlessly interesting city. A place with street life…it felt like home to me."

Home. I wish.

There are stories about the Victorian architecture and the world-famous Troy Music Hall, interesting shops and restaurants, arts and cultural initiatives, festivals in Riverfront Park, the Troy Farmer's Market, a new candy store. *Sigh.* I open another piece of taffy.

I click on a video about the city.

"If you have a dream for a small business, you can make it here in Troy."

"It's exciting to be a part of the rebirth of a noble, small American city."

Troy is on the eastern bank of the Hudson River and has a population of about 50,000. I scoff at my phone, thinking *A river is nothing compared to an ocean.* I continue reading.

It has close ties to the nearby cities of Albany and Schenectady, and, together, the three are called the Capital District.

Troy's motto is "Ilium fuit, Troja est," which means "Ilium was, Troy is." The name Troy, after the "legendary city of Troy, made famous in Homer's *Iliad*," was adopted in 1780. Troy became a town in 1791, then a village in 1801, then a chartered city in 1816. Once the fourth wealthiest city in the country, home of the detachable collar industry, and called "the collar city."

"How much longer, Dad?"

"Another hour."

I keep reading.

Troy is the birthplace of Uncle Sam, the iconic symbol of American patriotism. During the War of 1812, a Troy butcher named Samuel Wilson supplied barrels of beef to the troops. Wilson had several nephews working for him who joked that the barrels stamped "U.S.

Meats" meant "Uncle Sam's Meats." The name "Uncle Sam" caught on and spread among soldiers. Political cartoonist Thomas Nast created the Uncle Sam image decades later.

Oh, so Uncle Sam was a real person. I reluctantly admit to myself that is pretty cool.

Troy is home to the Emma Willard School, an independent preparatory school for girls. Founded in 1814 by American women's rights activist, Emma Willard, it was the first school in the country to provide girls with the same educational opportunities as boys. *The first one? Wow. Good for you, Emma.*

I check my messages, hoping for news of Salty. Nothing.

Rolling my sweatshirt into a pillow, I lean my head against the window for a proper nap.

"Willa, look," Sam says. "The river."

"Where are we?" I say, groggily. A green highway sign says "787 Exit 6A, Albany–Troy."

"We're here," Sam says. "There's the Hudson River."

I peer down at the brownish-green looking water, trees on either side. It looks narrow enough to swim across. No waves to speak of. No boats. No seagulls. No whooshing wind. I think of the ocean, vast and powerful. It could swallow this river for breakfast.

Sam senses my disdain and catches my eyes in the mirror for a second. He gives me a small smile and tilts his head as if to say, "Try to keep an open mind, okay?"

I look at the GPS gauge. We'll be at "Six Frear Park Lane" in ten minutes. We pass signs for Menands…South Troy…Hudson Valley Community College…Loudonville…Watervliet…Green Island…*There's an island here?* I think of Nantucket and Martha's Vineyard.

My mom wakes up. Checks the time. Takes out her makeup mirror and applies some lipstick. She reaches over and touches Sam's hand. He looks at her and smiles.

They are happy, excited about all of this. I sigh and fold my arms across my chest as Sam takes Exit 9E, Rte. 7 East, Troy–Bennington.

"That's Bennington, *Vermont*," Mom says cheerily. "It's only about a half hour from us. We'll take a drive up in October. They say the foliage is gorgeous."

The foliage is gorgeous in Bramble, too.

"What's that blue thing way up there?" I ask. It looks like a gigantic blue centipede or alien space ship towering above the trees, buildings, and steeples in the distance.

"I'm thinking a water tower," Sam says.

"Here's Hoosick Street now," Mom says brightly like she's a tour bus guide.

"Who's sick?" I ask sarcastically. *I'm sick. I'm sick of this place already.* There's a sign about Troy High winning some national sports title. *Whatever.*

Mom turns around. "We think you'll like Troy High school. They've got an excellent honors program. It might be an adjustment from Bramble, but I know you'll do great." She puts her hand on my knee for a second, before quickly turning around to call out another street name.

Bramble Academy. Tina, Ruby, Emily, Chandler—all my girlfriends—JFK and Jessie, Dr. Swammy, my other teachers. I remember how intimidated I was when I first started. The place looked like Hogwarts castle. There were uniforms, a strict code of conduct, and a contract signed upon arrival, pledging to use "superlative manners at all times, including in the classroom, on the playing fields, and in the dining hall." Everyone knows everyone by name; there are only 300 students in the whole place, pre-K to senior high. It was hard to break in, make friends, but once I did, it became like a second home. I can't believe I'm missing sophomore year, the sophomore soiree, the French club trip to Paris….I wonder who will run for student body president in my place? Tina said Ruby is considering it, mostly because it will look good on her college apps.

"Willa? Are you even listening to me?"

"What?" I shake myself away from the image of Ruby as leader of the sophomore class. "What, Mom?"

"We thought we'd settle in this weekend and then go visit the school on Monday, take a tour, meet the principal and some teachers, get you registered for classes."

"Whatever you want. It's not like I have a say."

"Willa, please," she says, softly. "Can you please just give it a chance?"

Sam finds my eyes in the mirror again. I remember how excited he is about his new job, so I decide to try; at least I can be civil to him and Mom. "I'm sure Troy High will be fine."

"I think it will be, sweetheart."

We pass a sign that says "Welcome to Troy, New York, Home of Uncle Sam."

"Hey, Dad," I say. "The city's named after you."

"That's right," Sam laughs. "You didn't know I was famous, did you?" I smile, the first time since we've left Bramble.

"Founded seventeen-eighty-nine," Mom reads the sign. "You're two and a quarter centuries old, babe. How are you managing that?"

"Perhaps I'm a vampire," Sam jokes. "I have some secrets, you know."

We head up Oakwood Avenue. *Oakwood*. That's a pretty name. Sounds like something out of an old romantic novel. I feel like we should be on the moors or heath or something like that.

"Here we are!" Mom says. "Frear Park Lane."

"*Fear* Park Lane," I say to be bratty. "Sounds awful."

"*Frear*," my mom overstates. "*Frear* Park Lane." She cranes her neck to read house numbers. "This is us! Number Six."

I get out of the car and survey the scene before me. A blue-shingled house with a wide front porch. There are balloons on the lamppost: a yellow smiley-face one and a silver one that reads "Welcome Home." I run my fingers up and down the ribbons. It was sweet of Donna to do this to make us feel welcome. It doesn't make this my home, but still.

I stare at the smiley smile, and it reminds me of a certain smiling dog. *Oh, Salty, I wish you were here.* I'd give anything to wrap my arms around that big stinky furry bear right now and have him smile at me.

I really could use a Salty Dog smile.

Chapter 14
Frear Park Lane

They must often change, who would be constant in happiness or wisdom.

—Confucius

I must admit, the house is nice. There's a guest bathroom off the foyer. The spacious living room has two couches, bookcases, a large fireplace, comfortable chairs and ottomans with reading lamps next to each, a piano, and a table for two with a chess board on top.

The dining room has a mahogany table, eight chairs, and a crystal chandelier. French glass doors lead to a more casual room with a television, leather sofas, a music system, more bookcases and shelves of board games, Scrabble Deluxe, Taboo…and lots of DVDs.

"Dr. Craig has quite a collection of classic movies," Sam says.

In the back corner of the house, there's an office with a large desk and a swivel chair.

"There's a second, smaller office in the attic," Mom says.

"You should take this big one, Stella," Sam says. "I have one at the college. Willa, come check out the kitchen."

Surprise! The kitchen is orange—*bright orange*—with white cabinets and appliances. It reminds me of Mikaela again — it's even brighter than her swimsuit.

"Gas stove," Sam says. "Great for baking." Sam knows how much I love his cakes and cookies. He makes the best double-chocolate chunk bars in all of New England; I'm sure of it.

There's a long black chalkboard like you'd see in a classroom. Sam points to a quote printed in bright yellow chalk:

I have a few splendid ideas which now only need proper incubation.
—Einstein

There is a message below it in a sprawling cursive handwriting in green:

~ Welcome Sam, Stella, and Willa ~

"An indoor Bramble Board of sorts," Sam quietly says to me. Sam and I worked on the Bramble Board together, and it had been one of my favorite times of the week, picking out quotes and writing them up with him. It would be great to have something like that again.

One whole wall of the kitchen is windows: a sliding glass door, cushioned window seats to the left and right, the afternoon sun streaming in. There's a couch facing out—a nice place to sit and read if anyone felt like reading. I walk to the door and look out. Sam and Mom come to stand beside me. A large blue jay lands on the birdfeeder, disrupting two little brown sparrows and setting the feeder swinging crazily. The squirrel on the ground below is glad for the shower of seeds. Sam unlocks the door, and we walk out onto the deck.

There's a patio table with orange chairs and matching umbrella. *Dr. Craig sure likes orange.* Off to the right are a grill and small vegetable garden. To the left is a stone fire pit with orange and gray Adirondack chairs encircling it. There are bright yellow, orange, hot pink, and red flowers —Dahlias, Sam says—and beyond that a sea of green, acres and acres of grass. "That's the Frear Park public golf course," he says. "That's one sport I never got into. You know what Mark Twain is supposed to have said about it?"

"What?"

"'Golf is a good walk spoiled.'"

We laugh.

"I used to love to golf," Mom calls out from the doorway. "How convenient. Maybe I can join a league."

Back inside the kitchen, there is a green wicker basket filled with fresh fruits, muffins and scones, tiny jars of assorted jams, granola, coffees, teas, and a note from Susan Scrimshaw, president of the Sage Colleges.

"I look forward to meeting her," Mom tucks the note back into the basket.

"She's quite impressive," Sam says as he takes a bite out of a mini muffin. "And has good taste in baked goods."

There's a bouquet of flowers from Sam's friend Donna Heald, with a note on college stationery saying not to worry about dinner as she has arranged for a local restaurant to deliver.

"That's Donna," Sam says. "Always so thoughtful. And modest. The letterhead says Provost. That's a promotion from dean. Good for Donna."

"Good for *you*, Sam," Mom says. "Now she'll have more power to keep you on." I try very hard not to roll my eyes at this, but I only half-succeed. I leave the happy, Troy-giddy couple and keep exploring.

In the center of the room is a long island with cushioned stools. There's a box with brochures about the area: Troy Music Hall, EMPAC, The Sanctuary for Independent Media, Capital Repertory Theatre, The Arts Center of the Capital Region... And there are three newspapers laid neatly on the counter: the *Record*, the *Times Union*, the *New York Times*. Mom picks up the *New York Times* and hugs it. "I was a *Boston Glober* by default on Cape Cod, but now that we're in the Empire State, I can get back to my *Times*."

According to Nana, growing up on Cape, Mom couldn't wait to move someplace more "cosmopolitan." She got her MBA from New York University, met and married my birthfather, Billy Havisham, in Washington, D.C. She's a city girl, through and through. I saw the draw of cities—we'd lived in a few I'd liked—but I hated the anonymity. Bramble is a true community, where people know each other, and watch out for each other, and support each other. How could a city ever give that to me?

"Come see the upstairs," Mom says. I follow her. "There are three bedrooms. We chose ours. Take your pick of the other two. And you'll still have your own bathroom, which I'm sure you'll appreciate." Stella was notorious for her long primping sessions.

I take the room farthest down the hall. The walls are a soft pale yellow with royal blue trim around the doors. There's a thick white brocade bedspread with yellow and blue throw pillows, and an oriental rug with the same colors over a dark brown hardwood floor. There's a desk with a brass lamp, a long cushioned window seat, a roomy closet, an old-fashioned looking tub in the bathroom.

I close the door and text Nana and Mum to let them know I arrived safely. I snap a few shots for Tina who made me promise I'd send her a picture of my room "right when you get there!" Things like that are important to her. It was really good of her and Ruby to buy all of those new clothes for me. Tina knows I'm not a shopper.

There's a knock on my door. "Your mom and I are going to the grocery store," Sam says. "Want to come?"

"No, thanks. I'm going to unpack."

"Okay, sure," Sam says. "And I just found bikes in the garage. Maybe you'd like to check out the neighborhood."

"Maybe. See you later."

I open up all of the packages of clothes from my friends. The dresser has five large drawers lined with a pretty yellow floral paper. Top drawer, underwear and pj's; second drawer, tops; third, jeans; then sweaters; bottom drawer, sweats and hoodies. I hang the nicer tops, skirts, dresses, and the beautiful, tailored tweed blazer from Tina, in the closet. My friends were so generous. The soft leather brown bomber jacket and matching boots from Ruby must have cost the Sivler's a fortune. I hope this isn't because they feel guilty about Salty running away from their spa that night. It wasn't their fault; Salty isn't a dog who likes to be cooped up. The Sivler's have enough to worry about right now. I make a mental note to send Ruby and her mom a card soon.

My suitcases feel like Hermione's bag; I can't believe I fit all these clothes in them. I pull out a jean jacket and think of Tina. She went overboard, as Tina always does. Extravagant is her middle name.

"I bought you all the fall fashion must-have's," she said. "And I made sure everything matches, so you sort of can't go wrong. You can wear this distressed jean jacket with everything: the suede fringe skirt, patterned bell bottoms, and faux fur vest. You're all set to impress."

I'm done unpacking my clothes, and I take a quick break before starting in on the next boxes. The window seat beckons and I sit, legs stretched out comfortably on the thick cushion, my back against the wall. Such a beautiful view and quiet...I can feel the Troy landscape try to work its magic on me.

But then Nana texts me back. Still no word on Salty. And just like that, all my anger and disappointment at the move returns in a swoop. *I'm not going to be charmed by some pretty trees*, I think fiercely at the window and jump up to keep unpacking.

In the nightstand drawer by the bed, there's a flashlight and a thick, old dictionary. I push them to the back and stick in a bag of Nana's candy. I would normally have a journal and pen here, too, but I still don't feel like writing.

I check out the bookcase—a Sue Grafton mystery, a Stephen King, a biography of Edith Wharton, a collection of Mary Oliver poems. I take Dr. Craig's books out and carefully stack them up on the shelf in the closet to make room for my own new mini-library. I put the new books the S's chose for me in alphabetical order by the author's last name, like I did at Sweet Bramble Books: Almond, Anderson, Appelt, Applegate... Which to read first?

I'm still trying to make a selection when I hear men's voices outside and return to the window.

Golfers. Spoiling good walks just across from my window. A man swings, shades his eyes with his hand to follow the arc of the ball, banters with his buddy, and then they hop into a little green and white golf cart and drive off up the hill. *Good riddance*, I think, unkindly.

I feel antsy, anxious. I need to get out of the house and stretch my legs. Maybe I'll go exploring. If we're going to be here awhile, I might as well start getting to know where the important things are. *Like this Library I've heard so much about.*

I brush my teeth and run a comb through my hair. I stick my phone in one pocket and some money in the other. Sunglasses? Check. Water bottle? Double check. I run down the stairs to go look for the bikes Sam found.

The shed behind the house is unlocked. There's a lawnmower,

rake and shovel, cross country skis, a toboggan, and three bikes. I choose the orange one—it's the easiest to get to, and I can't help but smile at anyone who has matching bikes and lawn furniture. The bike has a water bottle holder and a navy nylon sack. I unzip it to see what's inside: a bike lock with instructions, a map of Troy, coupons for "Sweet Sue's" and "Psychedelic Bagels." That was thoughtful of Dr. Craig. I think of the welcome basket President Scrimshaw sent and the flowers from Dr. Heald. People are nice in Troy.

Doesn't mean they're nicer than people in Bramble.

Frear Park Lane is a curious little street. There was no green metal sign on the corner like the other Troy streets we passed, rather a hand-painted wooden sign, "Frear Park Lane." I like the fact that it's different. *I wonder if one of the residents painted the sign*, I think as I start off down the street.

I bike slowly past a yellow house, and then a gray stone one set back from the street. I think I see someone in the window of the white colonial on the corner. I almost lift my hand to wave, but stop myself in time. *Traitor.* I glare at my arm before picking up speed and turning onto the next street. *Troy, I hope you're ready for me because here I come.*

Chapter 15
The Keys to the City

The happiest people I have known have been
those who gave themselves no concern, but did their
uttermost to mitigate the miseries of others.
—Elizabeth Cady Stanton

I bike past a restaurant on the corner, The Park Pub, with shamrocks on the sign. Customers are having lunch at tables on a large deck, shaded under green umbrellas. The sounds of conversation and laughter drift toward me along with the smell of burgers grilling. I pass by a little tan shed, golfers sorting out clubs. I think back to my conversation with my parents this morning. I only have vague recollections of my mom ever even talking about golf, so it must have been something she gave up after my birth father died. She always worked so hard while I was growing up; I spend so much time thinking about how much I hated moving constantly, but I forget that she didn't have time for community or fun either. *Maybe she needs a break from all that.* I want to fight against the thought, but it's hard. Mom and I don't always agree (probably because we're polar opposites), but I know she loves me. *Ugh, why do things have to be so complicated?* I sigh and keep biking.

On my left, I see a park with a playground. There are swings and sliding boards, little kids in bathing suits squealing as they run through water raining down from overhead sprinklers. An ice-cream truck pulls up with its cheerful recorded song. There's a group having a party, picnic tables laden with food, "Happy Birthday!" balloons and streamers, music blaring. I pause at the intersection. In front of me is water, probably one of the lakes Mom mentioned. Next to it is a brick building with a gray and red slate roof and chimneys. It's a beautiful building, but I don't want to be indoors right now. I put it on my mental list of things to check out later and keep pedaling.

I turn left and head down a hill. At the bottom, in the center of the roadway, is a blue and white fountain with red roses around it. Across the street, there's a formal flower garden and a pavilion with a green roof and white columns. *What an interesting place to have a park.* I slow down to take a closer look. *Right in the middle of things. There's a wedding.* I pause for a moment. The guests are seated;, the groom, ushers, and minister are standing. A limousine pulls up, doors open…bridesmaids in pale purple taffeta dresses…and now, the bride in lacy white. An older man in a tuxedo, probably her father, extends his arm and begins to escort her to the pavilion. A woman begins playing a harp, the guests rise….

An encouraging sign, a wedding on my first day here. A good omen for sure.

I don't usually like places like this, so perfectly manicured and controlled, but even I have to admit it's beautiful. It seems a lot of Troy agrees: I see people lounging and reading, couples strolling along the pathways, and many cyclists and hikers. *I bet Sam would like it here.* I can picture him with his leather journal opened up, pouring poetry out and into the sunlight. I leave the park before I can catch myself with any more Troy-friendly thoughts.

At the corner, I check the map, and turn left, heading down Oakwood Avenue, passing a red sign for St. Mary's Hospital. This is much different than biking in Bramble. Motorists are not very nice about making room. I've got to remember to buy a helmet. I go beneath an overpass, noting the vibrant mural of a red and yellow bird against a city backdrop. I then turn left on River Street.

I pass by the marina, more murals high atop brick buildings, a row of restaurants—Brown's, Malone's, Ryan's Wake, and Bomber's. Right past the bridge is another restaurant, Dinosaur Barbecue. The parking lot is packed. There's a cute statue, a guy about three feet high in a funky colored painted-on jacket. *Funky* is not a word you get to use all that often in Bramble. I don't give into my curiosity as I continue past.

In Riverfront Park, there's a Vietnam War Memorial, tall American flag, food vendors, people relaxing on the steps of an amphitheater. A little boy pushes a button and runs across a square as water spurts up from the ground at intermittent points. He is laughing hysterically. When the geysers stop, he smacks the button again, and runs, trying to anticipate where the water will be now. "Careful you don't fall," a woman calls to him from a bench where she's feeding a bottle to a baby.

I hop off my bike and walk up to the river bank. So this is the Hudson River.

There's a barge moving slowly and two boats with men fishing. I wish I could get close enough to dip my fingers in, but there are a cement barricade and a chain link fence. I sit on the ledge, close my eyes and take a deep breath.

It doesn't smell like the ocean.

It doesn't sound like the ocean, either. Too quiet. The ripples from the wake of the barge lapping against the barricade are nothing like waves against the jetty at home. It isn't babbling, though, like creeks always seem to do in books. The sound is hard to describe because it's mostly a lack of sound, but underneath there's…a sort of soft hum. I take another deep breath and try to sink into it.

Dun dun da dah! The loud sound startles me, and I turn to see a lady with stunning blue eyes, a small trumpet in her hand, smiling at me.

"Welcome, welcome," she says. She is tall and thin, with silvery hair, wearing a long blue dress that matches her eyes, a tan pouch hanging from a belt at her waist. A seagull lands near her feet, and she opens the pouch and throws down some crumbs.

I feel my eyes growing wide while I search for something to say. She beats me to it.

"Good afternoon, my dear. Allow me to welcome you to our fair city of Ilium…" More gulls alight and she feeds them, too. "Ilium," she repeats, "the grand Greek city of Troy."

Her wrinkled face is glowing. She is exuberantly happy. Leaning in toward me a bit, she studies my face with a look of intense interest, curiosity even. I look around nervously. She seems a little odd. There are several people near us, but none of them appear concerned. "Thank you." I manage a smile.

"You are heartily welcome, indeed." Her smile brightens. "And now, my girl…" her voice rises and eyes widen dramatically, "allow me to present to you the keys to our great city."

She holds out a ring with three keys on it.

"I don't understand," I stammer. "I think maybe you are mistaking me for someone else."

"Oh, no," she laughs, "I am quite certain you are *you*." She extends the ring closer to me. "Here take them," she nods encouragingly.

"But what are they for? And, I'm sorry, but may I ask who you are?" There's a deafeningly loud siren: *rrrrrr…rrrrr…rrrrr…beep…beep. beep…rrrrr…rrrrr…rrrrr…*, and I turn to watch as a long red fire truck barrels past: rrrrr…rrrrrrrrrr….

When I turn back, the woman is gone. *That's…strange.* I look around. There's no sight of her, but the key ring is dangling from the handlebar of my bike. I ask some people nearby if they saw "the lady in the blue gown with the trumpet," but none had. She's not someone I feel like you'd forget. *Where did she go?*

There are three keys on the ring —one silver, one gold, and one perhaps once brass now coated green with age. *What do they open? Who was that lady?*

This Troy place is getting interesting.

Chapter 16
Be Exactly Yourself

*Only in growth, reform, and change
paradoxically enough, is true security found.*
—Anne Morrow Lindbergh

Back on my bike, I continue past the green and gold "Uncle Sam Bus
Stop" and silver statue of a guy who I assume is Uncle Sam, where several
people are waiting for buses. I'm facing a triangular-shaped brick building
with the name The Market Block printed up top, and straight ahead, in
the window of a ground-level store, the word BOOKS. *Perfect.*

I cross the street and lock my bike to the rack. There's another
one of those funny little men I saw in front of the barbecue place. This
one is painted like a superhero, with a bright red cape billowing out from
his shoulders. *Hmmm.*

I head into the bookstore, trying to keep an open mind. It's hard
to live up to Sweet Bramble Books, which has the triple threat of books,
candy, and Nana. Other bookstores can't help it if they fall short. But
books are books, and this is where my people will be.

The inside of the store is bright and welcoming. Lots of comfy
armchairs, and a couple of couches have been scattered throughout,
begging me to plop down and crack open a new book. I resist,
remembering my stack from the S's back at home.

"Hello, there, welcome," a woman behind the counter greets me.
"How are you today?"

"Very well, and you?"

"Just ducky. May I help you find something?"

"No, thanks. I just moved here, today actually, and I was curious.
My grandmother owns a bookstore on Cape Cod…"

"Where on Cape Cod?" a man says, coming out of a back room
with a carton in his hands. He looks vaguely familiar.

"Bramble," I say.

"I know that store." He smiles. "I was there this summer. You sell candy, too, right?"

"Yes!" I clap my hands, elated at even this small connection. "It's called Sweet Bramble Books. Best books and best taffy, hands down."

"That's it," the man nods. "I stopped in to buy candy for a gift."

"I'm Willa," I extend my hand to shake his.

"Stanley," he says. "And this is Susan."

"Nice to meet you, Willa," she says, poking her head out from behind more boxes.

"Your grandmother and I chatted about the challenges of running an independent bookstore," Stanley says. "She's quite the bookseller. I went in to buy a box of saltwater taffy and came out with two books I could have gotten right here for free."

I laugh. "That's my Nana." I look around, admiring. "You have a really nice store."

"Willa just moved here today," Susan tells him.

"Welcome to Troy," Stanley says. "It's a great place. I think you'll like it here."

"I hope so," I say, not willing to admit it's already growing on me.

"Tomorrow's the Farmer's Market," Susan says. "It's right out the door there along River Street. Be sure to check it out."

"I'll tell my dad; he's really in to that sort of thing."

I keep moving through the store, stopping at different sections to see how they hold up to my high bookstore standards. Nana says it's important not to let personal biases keep good books out of a store. When I first started working at Nana's, I made a comment that the Science Fiction & Fantasy section was taking over some of my beloved realistic fiction, and maybe we didn't really need it? "Just because you don't like something, doesn't mean it isn't any good, Willa," was Nana's wise response. *I miss you, Nana.*

One book catches my eye in the biography section, under "New and Recommended." A blond woman is smiling confidently out at me: Kristen Gillibrand, United States Senator, *OFF THE SIDELINES, Raise*

Your Voice, Change the World.

"She lives here in Troy," says Susan, setting down a box and handing me the book. "She took Hillary Clinton's senate seat when Clinton became secretary of state; then she won a landslide election for a full six-year term."

"Wow," I say, impressed, "she looks so young." I read the back jacket blurbs, then open up the book:

"*My mom and my grandmother were two of the fiercest, most capable, bighearted, and original women I know. They created my frame of reference for women and work. And they taught me the bedrock lesson of life: Be exactly yourself.*"

Be exactly yourself. I like that.

"I definitely want to get this," I say, checking the price. "Would you hold a copy for me?"

"Sure," she says, grabbing a yellow sticky-note, "what's your name again?"

"Willa Havisham."

"Like Miss Havisham from *Great Expectations*?" she smiles.

"Well, hopefully not *too much* like her," I say, and we laugh.

She finishes up and puts my book in a growing stack behind the counter. "It'll be waiting here for you, okay?"

"Great! I'll be in tomorrow to pick up the book. And I'll bring my dad with me. He loves books, too. He's an English teacher and a writer. He's teaching at Russell Sage."

"What does he write?" Stanley asks, joining our conversation again.

"Poetry."

Stanley walks to a shelf and selects a book. "Your dad might enjoy this."

The Nightingales of Troy by Alice Fulton.

"And what does your mom like to read?" Stanley asks.

"Mostly business books."

"Is she Irish by any chance?" Stanley asks.

"Yes," I say. "Her last name is Clancy. Her grandparents were born in Ireland."

Stanley pulls another book. "She might like *The Irish Princess*. It's set in Troy."

"You've got to watch out for this one, Willa," Susan chimes in. "Stanley will sell you five copies of last year's phone book if you don't watch out."

"They don't even print phone books anymore," Stanley objects.

"Exactly," Susan says, and we laugh.

"Hold all three titles for me, please. We'll be in soon to get them."

"Here," Stanley says, handing me a sticker that says: **Enjoy Troy.** "A gift from us."

"Thank you." I slip the sticker into my back pocket and start to walk out before I remember something. "Oh, I meant to ask, what are the statues I see around town, the little men all painted differently. You've got one outside."

"The Uncle Sams," Stanley says. "There was a competition and various businesses and organizations sponsored artists to paint them with different themes."

"Uncle Sam is really big around here, huh?"

"Yes, indeedy," Susan says. "Sunday is the Uncle Sam Parade. We have it every year. It's quite an event. You and your family should check it out."

Maybe we will. I wave goodbye to Susan and Stanley, enjoying the fact that books can provide such an instant connection, even between complete strangers.

*****

Biking back home, I think of the line in that book: "Be exactly yourself."

That would have been perfect for the Bramble Board.

Chapter 17
Use Your Imagination

Yesterday I was clever, so I wanted to change the world.
Today I am wise, so I am changing myself.
—Rumi

My exploration continues, and I spy many more Uncle Sam statues. My favorite is one that's been painted black and white, like a piano keyboard. *I like that the contest is about individuality*, remembering the book I have on hold. But can I "be exactly myself" anywhere but Bramble? I'm still not sure.

I continue down Third Street, past a café called Spill 'n The Beans, a Greek restaurant, a clothing store, another café called The Daily Grind. At the corner, on the right, is PFEIL's Hardware store; on the left, a small corner park. A green and gold sign reads Summer in Barker Park. There we go with the green and gold again. I cross over, put my bike in a stand, and lock it.

Once in the park, I can see that the park is lovingly maintained, and there are whimsical whirligigs hanging from the trees. I smile at their bright colors and shiny streamers. I'm drawn to one extra-big, extra-bright, extra-shiny one. It's beautiful.

"I made that one," a girl's voice says from behind me. "I think it's the best."

I turn around to see three girls, all maybe nine or ten years old, looking up at me. I point up at the big whirligig. "This one?" She nods vigorously, grinning. She has butterfly barrettes on her massive crop of skinny braids, which look like they took someone a long time to plait so nicely. "It's very beautiful." The other two girls look at the ground. "They're all really pretty," I quickly add, and they're all smiling now.

"Where's your tiara and your sash?" asks one with red hair. She's wearing a pink t-shirt with movie princesses on it and colorful beaded bracelets from her wrist all the way to her elbow.

"What?" I ask, confused.

"John said one of the winners of the Uncle Sam Pageant was coming to talk to us about how she won," says the third girl quietly. She is stick-thin with straggly blond hair, dark circles under her eyes. She looks sad.

"I'm sorry, but you must be mistaken. I don't know anyone named John, and I've never won a pageant. I just moved here."

"But we've been waiting for you," Sad-eyes whispers.

"Today's the rehearsal for the parade," says Bracelets girl, fingering her bracelets.

"John said to wait here and you would come talk to us and maybe bring candy?" says Braids girl. She's chewing on the end of one of her braids, and all three are looking up at me, expectantly.

Well, this is all just getting curiouser and curiouser as Alice says. "Who's John?"

"He's always around here," Braids says, shaking her head at her friends. "I told you guys that didn't make sense because the Uncle Sam Parade's not until Sunday."

"Maybe he was talking about the homecoming queen at Troy High," Bracelets says. "John gets stuff confused sometimes."

"I told you John's crazy." Braids huffs and crosses her arms across her chest. She rolls her eyes at me. "So many crazies around here."

Sad-eyes slaps her arm. "Don't say crazy! It's mean." She looks back up at me and says, "John's just…."

"Different," Bracelets finishes for her. "And sometimes he forgets things. But he's nice." She elbows Braids. "Isn't he?" Braids shrugs.

"What kind of programs do they have here?" I ask, pointing to the Summer Events sign, trying to change the subject.

"Music and stuff," Braids says, "but that's done now that has school started."

"What do you like to do?" I ask.

Bracelets shrugs. "I don't know."

"You make bracelets," Sad-eyes says to her friend. "Show

94

her." Bracelets holds out her wrist, proudly showing off at least ten multicolored bracelets.

"Yes, I noticed them right away. They're beautiful."

"Thanks." She slides off one that's red, white and blue. "Here. You can have it."

"Really? Thank you." I slide it on to my wrist and hold it out for approval. "Do I look more patriotic?" They giggle.

"I've got lots of them," Bracelets says. "I made them for the Fourth of July."

"I love the parade," Braids says. "They give out candy."

"Is that the *only* thing you can think about?" Sad-eyes asks, exasperated now.

"What? I like candy," says Braids. "You like candy too!"

"My grandmother owns a candy store," I interject.

"That's amazing," Braids says. "I would never stop eating candy if I were you."

"It's a candy store on one side and a bookstore on the other."

"I have a book," Sad-eyes says, looking down and fiddling with a hole in her t-shirt. "A lady, she was an *author*, came here last summer and read the first chapter of a book she wrote. I asked for a copy because I wanted to read the rest, but I didn't have the money to buy it. After everybody left, she gave me one and said it was a gift. She wrote me a message and signed her name. Her *autograph*. I've read that book twenty-three, maybe twenty-four times. I can tell you the whole first chapter by heart."

"She can," Bracelets nods her head adamantly attesting to the fact, "no lie."

"I hide it under my bed so my brother won't steal it."

"He'll sell anything for weed money," Braids adds matter-of-factly.

This girl has only *one* book? And she has to hide it so her brother won't sell it for pot? I'm at a loss for words. No wonder this girl is so sad.

Braids shakes her head while Bracelets puts an arm around Sad-eyes, comforting her.

"I'm really sorry," I say, trying to think of some way I could help out.

Braids shrugs and crosses her arms again.

"I used to have a lot of books, but I lost them all," I say.

"How?" asks Bracelets.

"In a fire." The girls gasp. "But I was very lucky," I assure them, "because I had some friends who helped me start a new library." Something clicks in my mind: *I know how I can help!* "Do you three come here every Saturday?" The girls nod.

"Sure," Bracelets says.

"There's nothing else to do," Braids says.

I look them in the eyes. "I'm starting a club. A *book* club." Two of the girls clap their hands, but Braids is still unconvinced. I look for a picnic table but don't even see a bench. "We'll meet over there in the corner."

"What's it going to be like?" Bracelets asks.

"I'll bring books for us. We'll read for a while and talk, then have some candy."

"That sounds great!" Sad-eyes says loudly.

"How much does it cost?" Braids asks, flipping her hair over her shoulder.

"It's free."

"No way," Bracelets says. "Really?"

"Really." I'll get paperback copies of something at Market Block and bring some of Nana's candy. My wheels are turning excitedly. This is going to be *fun.*

"What's the club called?" Sad-eyes asks.

I shrug. "What do *you* think it should be called?" They look at each other and mimic my shrug. "Well, there we have our first assignment. Everyone come up with one or two possible names for our new club and we'll vote next week."

"We all get to vote?"

"Yes." I make sure to look each of them in the eye. I know how upset I've been in the past, knowing that I can't vote for things that are important to me. This club will be a true democracy.

Bracelets pipes up. "What about the key club? My sister's in key club at school—"

"Yeah, but that's not about books," Braids reminds her, not unkindly.

"We can definitely make that one of our options," I tell her. I think of the woman with the trumpet, from earlier. "That reminds me of something!" I run over to my bike and grab my pack. Bringing it back to the girls, I unzip the bag and take out the ring of keys. "Here. You can each choose one, but please bring them back next week."

"What do they open?" Braids asks.

"I don't know. A lady gave them to me. She didn't tell me what they open."

"Cool!" Braids takes the gold one.

"Maybe this one opens a candy store," Bracelets says, choosing the silver.

Sad-eyes reaches for the green one. "What do you think this opens?" she asks me.

"A castle? A secret garden? Use your imagination. What do you want it to open?"

She holds the key up closes her eyes. "I wish that this key will open the door to a *biiiiiig* house with a bedroom I don't have to share with anyone." She looks up at me. I don't know what to say, so I nod and smile at her. She smiles back.

"Maybe this gold one unlocks our clubhouse," Braids says.

"You mean what *should have been* our clubhouse," Bracelets retorts.

Sad-eyes fills me in. "There's this building up in Frear Park that used to be a fancy dance place when my grandmother was young. Now they keep lawnmowers there. But the mayor said it could be something else now, and he asked if anybody had suggestions."

"We did!" Braids says. "We said it should be a clubhouse just for girls. We wrote a plan for all the activities and events we would have. Talent shows and movie nights…"

"We even made a diorama showing what it would look like," Bracelets says.

"And outside, too," Sad-eyes says. "We were going to have a flower garden and a fish pond…"

"That sounds awesome," I say. "What happened?"

"There was a meeting," Bracelets explains. "And the grownups voted to make it a clubhouse for golfers instead."

"It wasn't fair at all," Braids shakes her head angrily. "We didn't get a chance to *vote*. We didn't even get a chance to talk."

Golfers over young girls?! Who would ever choose anyone over these amazing girls? I've known them for only a few minutes, but I can't imagine anyone ever telling them no; they're so sweet and determined. "I don't know anything about the building you're talking about. I only moved here today, but let me see what I can find out. Maybe it's not too late."

"Cool!" Sad-eyes says. "I have to go now."

I get on my bike.

"Wait," Sad-eyes says. "What's your name anyway?"

"Willa."

"Willa," Bracelets says. "That's pretty. I never heard that name before."

"Tell me your names," I say, and then suddenly change my mind. "Wait, don't tell me. How about each of you write a poem about your name and bring it to our first club meeting next Saturday." I tell them about Mikaela and the acrostic poem she wrote.

"She's got her own ice-cream stand?" Bracelets says. "How much money does she make?"

I shrug my shoulders.

"I don't know what to write about," Braids says.

"Write about the cookies you bake," Bracelets says, holding up her wrist. "I'm going to write about my bracelets. And how I'm so smart at math."

"You make the best cookies I've ever had," Sad-eyes says to her friend. "You could have your own business like that Mikaela girl."

"Then you better write about dancing," Braids says back to her.

"She's as good as J-Lo," Bracelets attests. "Wait 'til you see her."

Sad-eyes puts her hand over her eyes in a-don't-look-at-me embarrassed way.

"Wait 'til you see her, Willa," Braids says. "She's that good, for real."

"Are you going to bring a poem, Willa?" Sad-eyes asks.

"Of course! And I can't wait to hear all of yours. That's how we'll start our next meeting, okay? We'll share our poems."

"Good. I want to know all about you." She moves closer to me so her friends can't hear. "Can I please tell you my name now?"

"Okay."

"Cinderella," she whispers, not sounding very happy about that.

"That is a very nice name," I tell her, but I can see she's unconvinced. "It has lots of good letters for an acrostic poem."

She brightens. "That's true!"

I smile and wave as the girls bike out of sight. I bike as fast as I can; I've got some club planning to do!

Chapter 18
Who's Betty Friedan?

*The garden is growth and change and that
means loss as well as constant new treasures...*
—May Sarton

Consulting my map, I decide to head back to Frear Park Lane a different
way. I bike up Fifth Avenue, past brownstone buildings, lawyer's offices,
a donut shop called nibble inc., and restaurant called B Rad's Bistro. I
pass the First United Presbyterian Church. There's a rainbow flag like we
have at Bramble United Community. That means everyone is welcome.
Sometimes I think it's sad that we need to put up a flag showing we're
accepting, I'm happy to see it regardless.

Up farther, I turn right heading over to Sixth Avenue. There's a
bowling alley, Uncle Sam Lanes, *of course*, a small park with a big round
very tall apartment building. *A round building? I like it.*

At the corner, at the bottom of the last hill before Frear Park
Lane, I pause next to John Ray and Sons Fuel Company. There's a big red
friendly-looking dinosaur on top of the building. A man comes out. He
nods and smiles at me. "Hello there, young lady. How are you?"

"Fine, thanks, sir." People sure are friendly here in Troy.

As I begin biking up the hill, I immediately realize I have
underestimated this hill. This has to be the steepest hill in America,
maybe even the world. I switch to first gear and pump fast, passing what
looks to be an old bike trail on the left, then a school on the right.

By the time I reach Frear Park Lane, I'm sweating and exhausted.

I put the bike in the shed and head inside the house. Sam is in the
kitchen putting groceries away.

"There you are," he says. "I was beginning to get worried."

"Any news on Salty?" I ask, gulping down a glass of water.

"Not yet, Willa, sorry."

I hear my mom's voice on the phone in another room, mingling with the sound of the television. "How are you remembering 9-11?" The reporter asks her audience. She reminds us that Patriot's Day is a call for every person to do one act of service in our country. Mom's voice gets louder, more animated.

"Who's Mom talking to?"

"An old friend she reconnected with on Facebook. The woman lives here in Troy."

I walk down the hall. My mom has claimed the nice study off the living room as her office, and she's already started decorating, of course. The door isn't completely closed, so I stop outside to listen.

"That sounds great, Penny," she says. "I need to start exploring what I want to do next. I'm done with wedding planning. Too much drama, too many headaches. I'm thinking possibly financial planning. Something cut and dry. No self-absorbed debutantes acting horrified because one centerpiece has a wilted tulip…"

I walk up to my room. Take a shower. Check my messages. Still nothing on Salty. I text Nana and Mum about Cinderella and her friends, and the club we're starting together. They're both excited.

"I'm so proud of you!" texts Nana.

"Way to put your best feats forward! And on your first day!" comes in from Mum a few minutes later.

I'm lying on my bed, writing down book ideas for the club, when I hear the doorbell ring. It's a delivery man with dinner from a restaurant called the Knotty Pine. Spaghetti and meatballs, chicken Parmesan, a tossed salad, and garlic bread. I go downstairs and help carry the containers and plates outside to the table on the deck. There are people still golfing. I spot a little white golf ball on the grass.

"I wonder if they ever hit the house?" I ask.

"Let's hope not." Sam smiles. "So what did you do this afternoon?"

"I biked downtown. It's a quick ride. There's a great bookstore."

"Leave it to our daughter to find a bookstore on her first day in town," Sam says.

"She's always had a knack for finding them," Mom says with a smile. "I think Troy is going to be great for us. I was on the phone, reconnecting with a grad school friend of mine, Penny Miller. She read about the fire at the Inn and my business collapsing. Penny owns a yoga studio, and her husband Fred runs Kaleel Jamison Consulting Group. They have clients all over the world. Penny wants to help me get connected here in the Capital District. She invited me to a breakfast for local women philanthropists. An actress is doing a re-enactment of Betty Friedan's famous speech and—"

"Who's Betty Friedan?" I interrupt.

Mom looks surprised. "One of the most famous leaders of what's sometimes called Second Wave Feminism. She was fired from her job for being pregnant. Sigmund Freud…" My mom pauses. "You've heard of Freud, right?"

"Yes, Mom," I roll my eyes.

"Well, Freud had this theory that it is women's nature to be ruled by men…"

"*Ruled by men?*" I repeat.

"Freud obviously never met your mom," Sam interjects.

"You've got that right," Mom says. "Anyway, Willa, Freud was upset because he'd been studying women for thirty years and still couldn't figure out 'what women want.' Betty Friedan answered Freud's question with a book called *The Feminine Mystique*. She said that 'wife and mom' aren't the only roles for women; we have career interests, just like husbands and fathers do. Women want the power to choose what sort of lives we want to lead."

I nod, thinking about the girls and their clubhouse. They deserve that kind of power.

"Feminists like Betty Friedan and Gloria Steinem—" She stops and looks up at me. "You do know who Gloria Steinem is, right?" I shake my head ruefully. "Oh, what a shame," she continues. "Everything these women struggled for: equal access to education, equal pay for equal work, and your generation doesn't even know them."

"I think they teach women's history junior or senior year," Sam says.

"Women's history should be every year," my mom blurts out. "It was so stupid when I was in school, and we had 'Women's History Month' in March like that was the only time we should think about the contributions of women. We memorize the dates of every war; we teach what men were doing, with little anecdotal nods to the life of women."

"And hardly anything about teenagers, boys, and girls. It's like we don't count," I say.

"It's the same with Black History Month," Sam reminds us. "Minorities of all types have always struggled to find an equal voice. It's a shame because students miss out on a very big chunk of American history."

We all sit for a second, just thinking about this. *It's so frustrating.* I think back to the conversation I had with Sam the night of the fire when I told him I felt guilty being sad about JFK when there were girls like Malala in the world. I feel the same way now. There are *so* many things in the world I want to fix, so many people whose voices aren't heard; sometimes I feel overwhelmed by the amount of work that needs to be done.

Stop, Willa. I take a deep breath. *Remember what Sam said? You're an extraordinary person, but you don't have to fix all the world's problems today.* I return my focus to the table and see my mom smiling at me.

"Would you like to come to that breakfast with me? There will be lots of women leaders, many who will be focusing on stuff we've talked about. I think you'd like it."

I want to say yes, but I go with "maybe" instead. I'm not sure if I'm quite ready for one-on-one time with Mom. I scoop another meatball onto my plate.

I tell them about the books I have on hold for us at Market Block. "Senator Gillibrand lives here in Troy. I read a few pages from her book. I can't wait to get it."

"Elise Stefanik is from this area, too," Mom says. "The youngest woman to ever win a congressional seat. I think she was only twenty-nine." She takes another piece of garlic bread and lets out an exasperated huff. "I want to see more women in government. Men have screwed things up royally for too long."

"Ouch," Sam says. "Do I hear the beginnings of a campaign speech, babe?"

"We'll see," she says with a conspiratorial smirk. "No, honestly, I have no desire to be in politics. Business is my thing."

"How about you, Willa?" Sam says. "You have great leadership skills. You were going to run for president at..." He stops. Not wanting to bring up anything sad.

"Maybe you can run for a spot at Troy High." Mom looks up, unsure of my reaction. "It would be a great way to make friends."

I'm non-committal on this, too. I know I shouldn't hold a grudge, but I need another day or two to be angry with her. I think. But then I feel like I'm being petty, and I mull over how Mum and Nana always believe I can be the best version of myself. But then I remember Sam saying not to ignore personal feelings.

I decide to change the subject to something less confusing.

I tell them about meeting the girls in Barker Park. "They don't have access to a library right now, so I thought maybe I could start a book club with them."

"A book club, huh?" Sam nods with admiration. "I think that's a great idea, Willa."

Mom nods. "There are lots of ways to be in leadership. These girls sound like they could use a mentor, and I can't think of a better one." I think she's trying to make nice, mend some bridges, but then she turns the conversation another direction, and I'm not so sure. "Isn't downtown great?" she gushes. "Such impressive architecture, interesting shops and restaurants, exciting renovation projects along the river. Washington Park is a jewel. It's one of only two privately-owned ornamental parks in the country. The other is Gramercy Park in New York City. If we decide to stay in Troy, Sam, I think we should buy a brownstone, live on one floor, rent the other. It would be excellent income...."

What? She's already talking about buying a house here? I stand abruptly, pick up my plate and silverware.

"Don't worry," Mom says, "I've got the dishes." I don't respond.

"There's a house key for you on the counter by the flower vase," she continues. "And we started a list on the blackboard of things we need to buy."

Passing through the kitchen, I pick up the key and put it in my pocket. I think of the lady by the river this morning giving me those keys. Who was she anyway? I'll ask Stanley or Susan or maybe Cinderella. They should know.

Up in my room, I stretch out on the window seat and look out at that wide open sea of green. I picture my beautiful blue ocean.

I think about those girls in the park. How open and friendly they were; each with her own style and personality; how kind and supportive they were to each other; how welcoming they were to me. I twist the little patriotic-colored bracelet on my wrist. I think about Cinderella owning only one book. *This club is going to be so great.* I'm excited to hear the girls' poems and what sort of club names they come up with. I just know they're going to have some great ones.

I get back to my list of book ideas. What book to choose for our first meeting? Something short, but worthy; I call them "skinny-punch" titles. I think through my Willa's Pix list lost in the fire. *Charlotte's Web?* I love it, but they look like fourth or fifth graders; they've probably already read it. *Sarah Plain and Tall* is a quick read. No. I want something city girls can relate to more. I make a note to ask Susan or Stanley for some advice.

Four paperbacks shouldn't cost too much. I want to buy journals, too. I have enough money in the rainy-day fund from Mum and Riley. It would be even better if this club could turn into a reading and *writing* group. I remember when I got my first journal, how much I cherished my time writing in it. I want these girls to know that their voices matter, that there are people who want to hear what they have to say. I put "buy journals and pens" on my to-do list.

I check the Salty Dog Facebook page. Nothing.

I call Nana but get the recording.

I Google Betty Friedan and Gloria Steinem. Interesting stuff. Mom's right, it's awful that we don't learn about these women in school. It makes me wonder, *How many other important people have I missed because they were the "wrong" gender, or race, or religion?* I sign off, frustrated that I can't vote for something that has such a big effect on my life.

I think about how disappointed the girls were about not getting that city building for a clubhouse. They felt like no one even listened to them, like their voices didn't matter. *That's awful.* I look up Frear Park golf course and find news articles about the building.

A former gathering place for dances and other events, with fireplaces and a wide-open floor plan, it currently houses equipment for the Department of Parks and Recreation. Parks and Rec is moving to another location, and the mayor put out an "open call" for ideas from city residents. Claiming they would restore the building to its "former grandeur," the Troy Golfer's Association proposed a "country club-like lodge" for its members. A teacher named Patti Weaver, from PS 14, and Mary Jane Smith, founder of Unity House, spoke on behalf of "some local girls who had a great plan for the building," but, unfortunately, the girls hadn't registered in time to give their presentation at the meeting.

Just because they missed a deadline? I huff as I turn off the light and get into bed.

My final thought as I fall asleep is *I will find a way to help those girls.*

Chapter 19
Running with the Swans

For thy sweet love remember'd such wealth brings
That then I scorn to change my state with kings.
— Shakespeare, *Sonnet 29*

I'm awakened early the next morning by a very loud and annoying noise outside. I pull my pillow around my ears, but the sound drones on and on. I drag myself out of bed, go to the window and open the shade.

There's a man on a big red riding lawnmower cutting the golf course grass. He makes a turn at the border of this property, then heads back out again. *Must you mow so early?*

I walk down to the kitchen and put the tea kettle on. I investigate the welcome basket, choose a raspberry herbal tea bag and bran muffin, then sit on the couch and look outside.

A flock of seagulls lands on the golf course grass. Seagulls, in the city. The river does lead to the ocean like Sam said. Opening the sliding glass door, I step out to be closer to them. *Take me with you. Take me back to Bramble.* The annoying mower heads back in this direction, and on cue the gulls take off. *Goodbye.* I go back in as the kettle is whistling.

Three little black and white birds are nibbling at the feeder. A large blue jay, perhaps the same one from yesterday, lands and the small birds flee. *You need to stand your ground, little ones.* I wonder when I'll see a cardinal here in Troy. Cardinals always make me think of Gramp. After he died, I missed him terribly. It was January, snowing, and a bright red cardinal landed on a tree branch and stared right into my eyes. In that instant, I knew it was a sign from Gramp that he would always love me and be with me in spirit.

I look through some papers Mom left on the counter and find my registration paperwork. I wonder what Troy High school will be like? The guidance office reviewed my transcript and said I'd be able to "get up to speed" quickly, but I'm still nervous. I remember how it feels to burst into a new school in the middle of a semester, and it's not a feeling I ever wanted to revisit.

I can feel anxiety nipping at my heels, so I decide to go for a run. It always helps clear my head, and there's plenty of unexplored trails for me to choose from here in Troy.

Mom and Sam are still sleeping. There's no Salty Dog to walk. I close my eyes and send out a prayer. *Wherever you are, Salty, find your way to Nana.*

I put on my running stuff, leave a note, and head out. After turning right onto Oakwood Avenue, the road begins to rise. It seems this whole city is made of hills. I pass by a blue sign for the Martin Luther King Apartments, then a bit farther, tall wrought-iron gates and a green Oakwood Cemetery sign. There's a house on the right, perhaps the caretaker's, then on the left, a gray stone castle-like structure, like something out of medieval England.

There's a small blue marker with an arrow that says Uncle Sam's Grave. I veer right onto a paved path, thinking I'll make a loop around the perimeter. I jog at a smooth, easy pace, reading the names on headstones with dates back to the 1800's. Coming around a turn, I see a boy, maybe a year or two older than I am, jogging my way. As we pass, he smiles and nods, and I feel myself blushing. *Wow.* I try not to let him see how flustered I am. He is, in the words of Tina, a total hottie.

"Hey," he calls, stopping, jogging in place. I turn and tread to face him. He's much taller than I am, at least six feet, and I have to crane my neck to look up at him. But it's worth it; his smile is mesmerizing.

"Careful down by the lake," he says, "there's a crazy goose or duck, I don't know, maybe it's a swan mom trying to protect her babies. She nearly bit my leg off just now." He laughs.

I look at his legs, those muscles. His arms, those gorgeous brown eyes. I laugh nervously. *Don't go, don't go.* "Okay, thanks."

"See ya later," he says. "Have a good run."

"You too!" I watch as he runs off. I actually consider following him, but then reason rules and I keep running.

I hear footsteps coming up behind me. *Oh, I hope it's him again.*

"Hey, wait up," he says, jogging so close I can smell soap or cologne, deodorant, something. Beads of sweat are dripping from his forehead. He swipes them away. "You're that Cape Cod girl, right?"

"Yes," I steal a glance at him again. "How did you know that?"

"I didn't recognize you at first with your hair pulled back and that Red Sox cap on, but we're neighbors."

"Neighbors?" *Oh sweet Jesus halleluiah, as Mum would say.*

"I live in the white house on the corner," he says. "Dr. Craig told us you'd be moving in before she left. You should stop over sometime. My family would love to meet you."

"Okay, sure. Thanks," I mumble. "Um, what's your name?" *Very smooth Willa. Tina would be so proud.*

"Rob." He stops and holds out his hand. "And yours?"

"Willa." We shake hands, and I don't even try to keep the goofy grin off my face.

"Willa. I like that." My grin gets even bigger. "Okay, well, I'll leave you alone for your run. Watch out for the swan!" he yells as he jogs back down the path.

What does "sometime" mean? Sometime tomorrow? Sometime today? Sometime as soon as I get home and change? I start running again, picking up my pace.

As I approach a pond, a large swan comes squawking out toward me. Crazy swan mom, indeed. She is a formidable sight, and I'm glad Rob warned me about her. *That's not the only thing you're glad about.* I cut across the grass, in between headstones, coming out on a paved roadway.

I hear the sound of singing, and as I loop up around the hill, I see a large group gathered. One person is holding an American flag on a long pole, surrounded by men and women in military uniforms. In front of them, are two older men and two older women, dressed all in red, white, and blue. They're singing a beautiful rendition of "My Country, 'Tis of Thee." Marching back and forth in front of them is a man dressed up in a sparkly red, white, and blue outfit, like the cartoon caricatures of Uncle

Sam I've seen on TV. I hover at a distance, not wanting to be disrespectful or unpatriotic in my running clothes, sweating.

"What's going on here?" I ask a man in a black t-shirt with ARMY on it.

"A memorial service honoring the birthday of Uncle Sam. That's his grave there. We vets and other people come here every year on the weekend of the parade." He hands me a flyer. "Here."

"Thank you." I start jogging again. I really need some water.

I head back toward the entrance thinking about Rob. I can't believe he's my neighbor. This Troy place is getting more interesting by the minute.

Up ahead there's a man in a brown suit and hat crouching down by a grave marker. He stands, puts his finger tips to his lips, then reaches out to touch the stone. He kisses his hand again and touches the marker a second time. As I reach him, he turns to look at me. I pause. He has long thick sideburns like Elvis Presley or Hugh Jackman in *The Wolverine*. He tilts his head toward the grave stone. "They should be up there with me." He spits. "Foolish rules." He starts to walk then turns and points his finger at me. "Be sure to vote, young lady. Ain't nobody's fault but your own if you don't." He tips his hat, "good day," and walks off quickly.

That's odd. I move in closer to the simple graey headstone. The Uncle Sam hat symbol I see all over town is engraved on top with this inscription underneath:

Uncle Sam and Betsey Wilson's Children
DAUGHTER
Polly 1797–1805
Died from fever   Age 8
SON
Sam, Jr., 1800–1807
Died from a fractured skull
falling off a wagon   Age 7

Uncle Sam Memorial
Foundation 2011

Wow. Heart pounding, I look around for the man in the brown suit. *Was that Uncle Sam? The real man, Sam Wilson?* "They should be up there with me." *He wishes his children were laid to rest with him on the other side of the cemetery.* There are small urns on either side of the headstone with no flowers in them for Polly and Sam, Jr., not even the ugly plastic kind. I think of the fancy memorial for their father way on the other side of the cemetery.

Did I just meet the ghost of Uncle Sam?

Jogging back down Oakwood, I don't feel scared about talking with a spirit. If anything, I feel charged up, determined to do something.

Reaching Frear Park Lane, seeing the white house on the corner, where Rob lives, I smile again. If I weren't so thirsty, I'd probably giggle. Thankfully, no one's here to see the ridiculous grin that's back, and I continue to our house. I bound up the stairs and through the doorway. Water. I need water.

Mom and Sam are in the kitchen. "What are you so happy about?" Mom asks.

Way too much to tell you. "Nothing. Just had a good run." I tell them about Oakwood Cemetery and the memorial event.

"They really get into this Uncle Sam thing, don't they," Mom says.

"Well, I am an important national figure," Sam says, hands on hips like a superhero. "My day should be celebrated."

Mom smiles at him, grabbing a muffin from the welcome basket. "Oh, Willa, are you free tonight? The neighbors down the street invited us over for dinner."

"Which neighbors?"

"The Pryors, on the corner."

My heart beats faster. "In the white house?"

"Yes," Mom nods. "They're very nice. Gail is an engineer, a professor of Nanotechnology at Rensselaer. Ed is president of Pioneer Bank. They have two daughters, Desiree, away at college, and an adorable five-year-old, Josie, and a son, Rob; he's sixteen, I think he might go to Troy High. Gail was very friendly on the phone; maybe you can make a friend before your first day."

Rob is sixteen. That's really the only part I heard. Oh, that and *might go to Troy High.*

"Mom and I are going to check out the Farmer's Market downtown," Sam says. "We'll pick up the books you have on hold."

"Then we're off to buy a new computer and iPads," Mom says. "I know I'm spoiled, but I feel completely lost without my tech. What color do you want?"

"Pink, thanks. What time is the dinner?"

"Five o'clock," Sam says.

"Great. I'll be ready."

Mom and Sam look at each other and smile.

I take a shower and change into shorts and a t-shirt. I read the brochure the ARMY veteran gave me:

"The Uncle Sam Graveside Ceremony is a rich tradition. Since September 13, 1958, a group of veterans and citizens have honored Samuel Wilson on his birthday. The first Uncle Sam Birthday Parade was held in 1959, in downtown Troy. On September 15, 1961, the 87th United States Congress passed a resolution proclaiming Samuel Wilson of Troy, NY, as the progenitor of Uncle Sam; it was then signed by President John F. Kennedy."

JFK. Just seeing the name sends a pang of guilt through me. My phone beeps and I jump. It's Nana calling. "We're all still searching for Salty, honey. Don't worry. He'll turn up. How's Troy so far?"

"Um…it's okay…," I say as I pick at a loose thread on the blanket. "It's really different from Bramble, but I think it could be a good different. Oh, and I met a neighbor. A really nice boy named Rob," I sneak this last part in, rushing the words together.

"A new friend already?" I can hear Nana's eyebrows go up, even over the phone, but she doesn't comment further. She says, "Good for you, honey. Can't wait to meet him."

"When are you coming to visit, Nana?"

"As soon as I find Salty."

Chapter 20
The Characters

I'm not going to change the way I look or the way
I feel to conform to anything. I've always been a freak.
—John Lennon

I choose a pair of pink and brown swirled leggings and a lightweight brown peasant blouse from the "Tina and Ruby Fall Collection," smiling as I tie up my pink Chucks. I'm sure Tina would have quite a few things to say about my choice of footwear, but there is no way I'm going to this dinner without my trusty sneaks.

I put on some lip gloss—Juicy Grapefruit—also courtesy of T&R, and fix my hair. I try something new, crunching up my curls all the way around, instead of my usual asymmetrical 'do. *Maybe I'm getting better at this change thing.* A hairstyle isn't the same as a cross-state move, but it's still something.

I find a pair of pink and brown earrings in the box of jewelry from yet another Bramble friend; they go great with the blouse. I wonder if Tina took everyone shopping or texted the whole group a color scheme. I wouldn't put it past her. I check out the different scents in the Victoria Secret bag and choose the one called Perfectly Pink. I put on my new red, white, and blue bracelet. Even I can see it doesn't really go with the rest of the outfit, but it feels right, and that's enough for me.

"You look nice, Willa," Mom says when I come downstairs.

"Thanks," I say. "You, too." She's wearing a fitted red sundress, oversized sunglasses nestled on top of her head. She looks relaxed, happy. I blink when I realize how long it's been since I saw her like this. In my mind, I think back to another talk I had with Sam, right after the fire, when I was absolutely seething with anger at her. *Stella works hard, harder than any of us realize, Willa. She deserves some time for herself.* I didn't want to listen to him then, but seeing her now makes me question past-Willa's judgment.

"Here's your pink iPad," she says, handing me a bag, "and Sam's got your book."

"Thanks, Mom," I say, giving her a quick hug.

"Thank you, Willa." She seems so surprised and grateful for the gesture. I resolve to make an effort to be nicer to her. *The fire couldn't have been easy on her, either*, I remind myself.

We head down the street, Mom carrying a bottle of wine, Dad carrying a bag of apples from the Farmer's Market, and me carrying one of the bags of candy from Sweet Bramble Books. We pass the yellow house, and the gray one set back from the road, still no sign of anyone, butterflies rising as we reach the Pryor's.

Both parents welcome us at the door. *I can see where Rob gets his looks.* Mr. and Mrs. Pryor are a stunning couple. He's tall, like his son, broad-shouldered, with that same brilliant smile. Mrs. Pryor's good looks would be almost intimidating—sharp cheekbones and sculpted arms—if it weren't for the twinkle of mischief I see in her eye.

"Come in, come in," she says, ushering us through a high-ceilinged foyer, directing us toward the backyard. "I hope you like salmon," she calls over her shoulder. "If you don't, we'd be happy to grill some chicken. Or veggie or black-bean burgers."

"Salmon's great for us," Mom replies. "Thank you, Gail."

I feel a small hand tugging at my arm, and I look down to see a little girl in a sparkly pink dress with matching cowboy boots. "My name is Josie," she says, very serious. "Can I show you something?"

"Josie has been waiting all day to show the new girl her newfound skill," says Mr. Pryor with a laugh. "I hope you don't mind."

I look straight at Josie and say, "I would be honored."

Her face lights up with a huge smile. She twirls around once and then pulls something out of the hallway. "Stand back a bit please," she says to me, then starts hula hooping, staring at me the whole time to be sure I'm noticing. The show lasts several minutes. The grown-ups laugh and clap.

"Very impressive," I say. "You are the best hula-hooper I have ever seen."

"Have you seen a lot?"

I nod, extra-serious, and then flash her a grin. She giggles. "I like your sneakers," Josie says, taking my hand. "Come on." She leads me through their house and out into the backyard. "This is my favorite part of our house," she gestures to the whole backyard. "I like it even more than my princess bedroom."

I can't blame her. The Pryor's have put a lot of time into their yard and it is absolutely beautiful. There are flower beds holding blooms of every color, at least a dozen trees, including two that look like they might have been there when the real Uncle Sam walked these streets. A tire swing hangs from one, and a hammock is strung between them.

"You have a lovely home, Mrs. Pryor," I say.

"Oh, please, call me Gail. And thank you. Have you seen the vegetable garden? It's my husband's pride and joy."

She walks me over to the side yard and, sure enough, Mr. Pryor is beaming over rows of vegetables while talking to Sam. "We added three varieties of kale this summer," he says proudly. Mrs. Pryor—*Gail*, I remind myself—runs her hand over the crinkly green rows.

"All Hail mighty kale," Sam jokes.

"Booted poor broccoli right out the door," Mrs. Pryor says, and they laugh.

"Insider vegetable jokes," Rob whispers in my ear.

I spin around, suddenly very aware of how narrow the side yard is. "Rob! Hi?"

"You two know each other?" Gail asks, glancing at us.

Before I can stammer something out, Rob swoops in. "I saved Willa from a killer swan this morning." He smiles down at me, and I feel my goofy grin resuming its reign over my face.

"Come on, Willa," Josie elbows me. I snap out of my trance. All four parents are watching us. "Time to eat," Josie takes my hand again.

There's a yellow and white striped awning over a brick patio, colorful ceramic pots of flowers all around. The table is beautiful, set with bright yellow plates and red, yellow, and orange striped napkins, small bouquets of daisies in cut glass vases.

"You sit next to me," Josie says, patting the seat.

"Okay, thank you."

"Josie must like you, Willa," Mr. Pryor says. "That's Dezi's seat. Josie won't let anybody else sit there."

"*Dad*," Josie scowls. "Do you not see me? I'm right here. I can tell her myself."

"Yes, you can, sweetheart. Sorry." Mr. Pryor smiles at me over a water glass.

"You don't ever want to mess with Josie," Rob says. He's sitting across from me. I smile and take a sip of water, just to have something to do with my hands. I'm grateful when Gail comes out with the first course.

"Thank you," I say, taking a helping of a delicious looking spinach and feta salad.

"Make sure you take some strawberries to put on top," she says, handing me a small dish. "Rob grew these himself." I smile.

"I like your bracelet," Josie says. "Where did you buy it?"

"A friend made it for me."

"She should make you a pink one to match your sneakers."

I spin my red, white, and blue bracelet around on my wrist for a second before answering. "That would be very kind of her, but I wouldn't stop loving this one. It's okay if not everything matches." Josie looks slightly unconvinced, but not for long.

"Can she make me one, too?"

"I'll ask her."

"Could you ask her to make us matching ones? Then it wouldn't matter if our bracelets matched our shoes because we'd match each *other*."

Rob laughs and shakes his head. "Josie, let Willa eat."

"What a beautiful home you have," Mom says. "How long have you lived here, Gail?"

"Twenty years. We love it here."

"It's a great location," Mr. Pryor says. "The YMCA is right up the street. No excuse for not exercising, but I manage to find ways."

"The Zumba classes are awesome," Mrs. Pryor says to Mom. "My friend, Emilly, teaches on Fridays. She's from Kenya, and she's a chemistry professor at Sage."

"Do they have a good track?" Mom asks, always the runner.

"They do! You a runner?"

Mom nods. "Willa and I both run."

"You'll have to do the Turkey Trot with us in November," Mrs. Pryor says. "It's Thanksgiving morning—a big Troy tradition."

"Justifies all that pie later," Mr. Pryor jokes.

Mom and Dad look at each other and smile. I can tell they like this family.

Mr. Pryor brings the grilled salmon to the table and serves us. "The pesto marinade is Gail's specialty," he says proudly. "The basil is from my garden."

Mrs. Pryor passes around a bowl of cheese tortellini with sliced red and yellow cherry tomatoes and fresh herbs.

"This is delicious," Sam says.

"I'm in heaven," Mom says. "Thank you so much for inviting us."

"Our pleasure," Mrs. Pryor says. "We're glad you could join us."

"Are you from Troy?" Sam asks.

"Michael and I met in college," Mrs. Pryor says. "I was at Russell Sage, and he was at R.P.I."

"They call it *Rensselaer* now," Mr. Pryor says. "Still haven't gotten used to things changing names." Mom nods and Sam gives him a knowing look. *I'm not the only one who doesn't like change.* Gail continues the story of how they met.

"We met at The Ruck, a college hang-out," she says. "It was Trivia Night." She smiles at her husband. "Go ahead, babe. You tell the rest of the story."

"My trivia team was undefeated in the Capital Region," Mr. Pryor says, puffing out his chest. "We were golden. Tuesday night, Bootlegger's, Wednesday night, Finnbars, then one Thursday at the Ruck this new team from Sage signs up. I took one look at her,"—he points to his wife—"and I was a goner. She's gorgeous and then she starts talking, and I find out she's smart and funny, too? Well, I drove straight to the jewelry store for a diamond."

"Really?" I say. "That's so romantic."

Rob laughs. My face reddens.

"Well, not that night," Mr. Pryor says, "but pretty soon after that."

Sam looks at my mom and smiles. They love each other that much, too.

"How did you and Sam meet, Stella?" Mrs. Pryor asks my mom.

"Willa set us up on our first date," Mom says.

"She's quite the matchmaker," Sam says.

"And wedding planner," Mom adds. "And writer. She's going to be an author."

I look quickly at my mom. Her face is shining with pride. I smile at her and then she winks at me.

"A writer, huh?" Mrs. Pryor says. She smiles at her son. "Rob is an aspiring filmmaker. Tell the Gracemores what you're—"

"*Ma*," Rob says, shaking his head like "don't start talking about me."

"I'd love to hear more," I say.

"Sure, later," he mumbles.

I take another bite of pasta, trying to ignore the fact that all four parents are staring at us again.

"That was divine," Sam says as we're finishing our food. "I have to get those recipes from you."

"Do you cook?"

"Sam's a very accomplished chef." Mom laces her hand through his arm. "We are two lucky girls."

Gail's eyes brighten. She's excited to have found another foodie. She launches into a conversation about herbs and cooking techniques. Rob kicks my foot under the table, and my eyes dart to his.

"Mom can go on about cilantro versus parsley for hours. We

should probably make a break for it before they rope us in. You play bocce?"

"Yes," I nod. "I love it."

"Great," he says. "Let's go."

There's a bocce area set up in the middle of the yard.

"What color do you want, Willa?" Rob asks. He's bending over the set, giving me a perfect view of his perfect arms.

Any color. Who cares about colors? "Green, please." Thank goodness he doesn't read minds.

Rob gathers the green balls and lays them on the grass by my feet. "Here you go."

A flash of orange fur dashes by in a flurry. "That's Garfield," Rob says, shaking his head, laughing. "He thinks he's a hunter, but he's scared of butterflies."

"Aw, poor guy. He's just too sweet to hurt them." I take my first throw, getting pretty close.

Rob laughs. "He's a scaredy-cat." His ball hits mine, nudging it out of first place. *Drat.* "So, how come you left Cape Cod?" he asks.

I tell him about the Inn and losing Salty Dog.

He touches my arm. "I'm sorry, Willa. That's a lot to deal with." He stares into my eyes with real compassion. He taps my hand. He smiles. "Don't worry. Your dog will turn up. You've got to keep believing that."

"Thanks." I focus on the game and Rob gives me some space to get a handle on my emotions. *Hear that, Salty? You've got to come back so you can meet all these new people.* I send up another prayer that he'll be found soon.

"So what do you think of Troy so far?"

I begin at the beginning, telling him about the lady in the blue dress by the river this morning who welcomed me to the "grand city of Ilium" and gave me a ring of keys.

Rob laughs. "So you've met one of the town characters."

"The characters?"

"That's my name for them," he says. "Some people call them

'the crazies.' My sister, Dezi, calls them 'wackadoodles.' To me, they're interesting characters. Troy's famous for them. You meet them on the street, and they start talking to you. Some are homeless, some have mental problems, and some have addictions. There are veterans still haunted by war, and old people with dementia. Most are poor, and some are lonely, and they need someone to listen to them. I like talking to them, hearing their stories."

"Is your film about these 'characters' as you call them?"

"Yep. They make great subjects because they're so...." He searches for the right word. "Dynamic. And they don't really have anyone out there, listening to them, telling them their voices matter." His voice gets quieter like he's shy about what he's saying but he keeps going. "I think it's important that everyone has a chance to have their voice heard. It makes people feel good, knowing that they matter to someone else."

Josie comes running up with her hula hoop, breaking us out of the serious moment. "Josie, please, no! No more hula hoop!" He's holding his head in his hands, acting distraught, but I can hear the teasing in his voice, and Josie just grins and keeps on hooping. "Can you go find Garfield? I'd like to introduce him to Willa." As suddenly as she appeared, she's off like a flash.

"She is adorable."

"That's one word for her."

We go back to the game, and I think some more about his film project. "Is it a documentary?"

"A documentary with soul. I promise you it won't be boring."

"I can't wait to see it."

"It's still too rough," Rob says. "But, sure, I'll show you when I'm ready."

"Do you ever worry about your safety? Like what if someone followed you home?"

"So what if they did? I invited a guy home for dinner last winter. He was panhandling by Walgreens on Hoosick, and it was freezing out. I'd seen him the day before, and I stopped and gave him half a sandwich.

122

'Thank you, sir,' he said, so polite. Nobody calls me 'sir.' The next night we were driving home, and there he was again, shivering, snow collecting on his beard. I asked Dad to stop. I went up to him and said, 'Hi, I'm Rob.' He said his name was John, and he asked me, 'Did you bring me another sandwich?' I said, 'No, but do you want to come to my house for dinner?' John said the lasagna was 'almost as good' as his mom used to make, but it needed 'more garlic.' After dessert, I drove with Dad to take John downtown to a homeless shelter called Joseph's House. I volunteer there sometimes; it's a really good place."

Wow," I say. "I love that you did that." I tell Rob about the girls I met at the park this afternoon.

"My mom doesn't like that they took the benches out of that park," he says. "It's near a soup kitchen and the characters congregate there. Now they can't even sit down. They need somewhere to go. Not everyone has a yard like this," he waves his hand around, "to hang out with friends. Barker Park was a place where they could meet and converse. They have as much right to be there as everybody else."

I take another turn throwing my bocce ball, stealing glances at him as I do. *Attractive, funny,* and *cares about his community? Talk about the whole package.*

"I'm sorry about the benches. I don't like it when people try to keep others out, either." I tell Rob how angry I got when the homeowners' association on the Cape decided only the "right people" should be able to use the beach. "They passed out flags for 'residents only' and you were supposed to stick that flag next to you in the sand so that the patrol guys would know you belonged. I refused. Beaches should belong to everyone."

"I like a girl who speaks up. Even if she does beat me at bocce ball."

"Best out of three?" I toss the ball in the air and catch it.

"You are on."

Chapter 21
Smitten

You can't stay in your corner of the Forest
waiting for others to come to you. You have to go to
them sometimes.

—A.A. Milne, *Winnie-the-Pooh*

"I can't hold Josie off forever," Rob reminds me. "The rematch must happen now."

"Sure." I laugh. "If you're ready to lose."

"Confident, are we?" He scrolls through his iPhone. "You okay with hip hop?"

"Sure."

"What music do you like?" asks Rob.

"Pretty much everything. Rap, rock, country, pop…mostly pop."

"Pop, huh?" Rob smiles. "That's okay. Some of it's good."

"Ladies first." He hands me the little white ball. I toss it a good distance away, then follow with my first green ball. It lands about a foot away.

"Nice shot," he says. He lobs a red ball overhand, smacking my green one way out of range.

"So that's how you want to play, huh?" I joke, picking up my second green ball. It lands even closer than the first.

We keep playing, neck and neck. "So can I assume from your hat this morning that you are a Sox fan?"

"Red Sox Nation, baby. What about you?"

"New York all the way. Giants, Yankees, Knicks."

"I like how the other three rhyme," I say, "the Nets, the Mets, and the Jets."

"The rhyming was intentional," Rob says.

"Really?"

"You're a funny girl. Gullible. I like that. Cute."

I think you're cute, too. I grab at any topic to distract myself from his gorgeous brown eyes looking down at me. "Where do you go to school?" *Troy High? Please say Troy High.*

"I wanted to go to Troy High, but my Dad went to Albany Academy, and he's so proud of that place. It meant a lot to him for me to go there, too."

I throw my next shot wide, bummed by his response. "What year are you?"

"A junior. How about you?"

"A sophomore. And your sister, Desiree. Where's she?"

"Dezi's a freshman at Siena College. She could commute. It's only a half hour away, but she wants the 'total college experience' as she says."

"I would, too. What's her major?"

"Double major. International Studies and Leadership Development. She's got an awesome voice, too, writes her own songs, plays the guitar and the piano."

"She sounds awesome."

"Dez'll be home for her birthday next month. She'd love to meet you. She and Mom and Dad all have October birthdays. We do this big Everybody's Birthday Party. It's crazy. They invite tons of people, always have live music, great food...I think this year the Park Pub is catering it."

"That's the Irish place down the street."

"Yeah. They've got the sickest chicken wings. Peanut butter and jelly are the best."

"Peanut butter and jelly? That's an...unusual combination for wings."

He laughs again. "Hey, don't knock it 'til you try it. I'll make sure you're invited to the party, and you can apologize to the wings personally."

"Well, I hope they can forgive me."

"I'm sure you'll find a way to convince them." He throws again, just missing my ball. "The party's a lot of fun. They have a huge birthday cake and everyone swaps presents."

"I'm a bit jealous of your big family." I tell him how it was only me

126

and Stella for years.

"Well, you can always take some of my family. There's more than enough to go around. But seriously, the party's a blast. It's probably my favorite day of the year. Mom even hires a DJ. My parents love to dance. If you play the Cupid Shuffle at your house later, they'll hear it and come running up the street to join you."

"What's the Cupid Shuffle?"

"What?" Rob is surprised. "You don't know the Cupid Shuffle?"

"Is it a line dance, like the Macarena?"

"Oh...*no*," Rob shakes his head, adamantly. "Don't even whisper Macarena around my Mom or she'll go off about it being white people's sorry excuse for a dance."

A woman laughs. Mrs. Pryor is standing behind us. "There's not even hips or bootie involved," she says to me. "Now the Cupid Shuffle? The Electric Slide? The Wobble? That's real dancing."

Rob looks at me. "Don't worry. Dez or Josie will give you a lesson before the party."

"Teach her yourself, Rob," Mrs. Pryor says.

"Ma," Rob cautions.

"Willa, trust me," she smiles, "this boy can dance."

"Mom, stop." He's actually covering his face with his hand, and I can't help but smile.

"Don't be shy, Son," she says. "You know you've got the moves."

"C'mon, Mom."

"He really ought to go by his middle name, Michael." I look at her blankly. "*Michael Jackson*," she says.

"Mom," Rob says, unable to handle his embarrassment anymore. "Go."

Mrs. Pryor laughs. "Okay. I'll leave you to finish your game. Then come join us for dessert. I was going to bake, but Rob insisted on treats from The Cookie Factory."

"Fudge fancies, right?" Robs says.

"A whole dozen just for you, son."

"Fudge fancies?" I ask.

"It's a vanilla sugar cookie with a big glob of chocolate on top. Wicked sick."

"Sounds delicious."

"Okay," he says, turning his attention back to bocce. "What's the score?"

"Ten-eight, you," I say, "and you're up."

He scoops up a red ball. The muscles on his long dark arms are smooth and chiseled. He throws it in a high arch. It plunks down inches from the white ball.

"Niiice," I say.

"Thanks. You're up. For the win. No pressure, Willa."

I ignore him as I pick up my ball. "What sports do you play?" I ask.

"Right now, soccer," Rob says. "You should come to one of my games."

"I'd like that," I say. "What position?"

"Center mid. Then basketball in the winter. Track in the spring. And you?"

"I used to play soccer, but now running's my main thing."

"At Troy High you can do cross country now, indoor track in the winter, outdoor in the spring. They've got a wicked strong team."

"I hope I like the school. I'm nervous about starting in the middle of the semester," I confess.

"You'll be okay. I've got lots of friends there. They say the food's no good, but other than that, people like it there. Do you know who your teachers are yet?"

I shake my head. "Well, I know, but I don't remember. I got my list of classes only a few days ago." I don't add that I was so angry about moving that I refused to even pay attention to any of the information they gave me. I can't believe how different I feel now from how I felt then. *Maybe it's the magic of Uncle Sam.*

"Here he is," Josie comes up to us, struggling to carry Garfield, who weighs more than she does.

"Oh good, Josie, thanks," Rob smiles, winking at me. "Willa, this is Garfield." I scratch his head, and he stops squirming and purrs. "Garfield is a very good judge of character. Aren't you buddy?" Rob scratches under his chin, and Garfield closes his eyes, in cat heaven. "Josie, can you bring Garfield in the house now? He's probably really thirsty." We watch her sashay off in her pink cowboy boots.

"Any requests?" Rob asks, flipping through songs on his phone.

"Hmmmm...what about Little Wayne?" I pick up my last green ball, aim, and toss.

Smack. It hits one of his red balls, knocking it out of scoring range.

"Sweet," he says, picking his newest song. "I heard he's coming to the Jazz Fest this year."

I look at him, eyebrows raised. "Jazz Fest?"

"Oh man, the Jazz Fest is the best. It's two days, at the Saratoga Performing Arts Center. My whole family goes, all my aunts and uncles, cousins. We get there early Saturday morning, set up a tent, eat great food, and listen to music 'til midnight, then do it all over again on Sunday."

"I've never been to a jazz festival. It sounds like fun. When is it?"

"August. Your family'll have to go with us next year."

Next year? He's thinking that far ahead? I let that idea hang there in the air between us for a minute, shocked and warmed by it, all at once. *I only just met you, Rob, and August is a year away....*

"Definitely," I say, surprising myself. *Who are you, and what have you done with Willa?* I ask myself.

We finish our final game and Rob wins, but only by a point. We put each other's numbers in our phones.

"I've got practice after school all week," Rob says, "but maybe we can go for ice cream one night if you want. There's a place called the Snowman in Lansingburgh."

"Sure. I love ice cream."

"Good." He tucks my hair behind my ear, and his fingers brush against my cheek.

Chapter 22
A New Tradition

Change does not roll in on the wheels of
inevitability, but comes through continuous struggle.
—Martin Luther King

Early Sunday morning, I put on shorts and a shirt, lace up my running sneaks and head downstairs. I check the directions to Troy High School and go for a run to check it out.

All's quiet on Frear Park Lane. I look up at the second-floor windows of the Pryor's house. Which one is Rob's, I wonder? On Sundays at home, we'd be going to BUC, Bramble United Community, a spiritual gathering place for people of all faiths—Christian, Jew, Muslim, Hindu, Atheist, Agnostic; It doesn't matter what you believe, it matters how you act and what you do. We celebrate and share gratitude to God—however we imagine God to be. I hope we can find somewhere just as special here in Troy, but for today, I choose to use my run to give thanks.

At the corner, I turn left on Lavin Court. Whoever lives in that house there planted sunflowers on both sides of the sidewalk, so they form a sunny canopy around you as you pass. What a nice idea. It reminds me of Mum's sunflowers, the sunny path that would lead me to her. She would love this. I remember the seeds she gave me. I will plant them today. I'm sure Dr. Craig would love a sunny addition to her yard.

I turn left on "Who's Sick" Street, quiet this early on a Sunday morning. Turning right onto Burdett Avenue, I pass Samaritan Hospital, The Eddy, signs for the RPI Fieldhouse, Troy Middle School, and then there it is—Troy High School—"Home of the Flying Horses," a three-story butterscotch colored brick building, almost as long as a Bramble block. The school seal is purple and gold. A tall American flag waves proudly in the breeze. I make a wish, starting to feel excited about school.

*****

Back home in the kitchen, I pour a glass of water and read Mum's directions for planting the sunflower seeds. I find hand tools and gloves in the shed. *Now, where to plant?* I find a perfect spot, just on the crest of a slope, toward the back of the yard. They'll have room to grown nice and tall, and you'll be able to see them from the house.

The ground is hard, so I haul over the hose to wet the dirt and loosen it. I plant the seeds to the depth instructed, cover with soil, then water the top.

"So my daughter's got a green thumb now, huh," Sam says, coming up behind me.

"I like it when you call me your daughter, Dad."

"Thank you, Willa." He hugs me.

We stand there for a minute, looking out over the golf course. A golf cart descends from the hill by the Park Pub, then another and another and another lining up in a row. "Must be a tournament," Sam says.

I make a cup of ginger tea to take up to my room. I find a box of blank notecards in the desk, thoughtfully left by Dr. Craig. I write to Mum and Riley to ask how they're doing, telling them how I'm putting the rainy-day money to good use for books and journals for the Key Club girls, and how I just planted the sunflower seeds.

I write a note to Ruby asking how her mom is doing with the cancer treatments and telling her I heard she's running for class president. "Good for you, Rube. We need more women in political office." I suggest that she read *Off the Sidelines*.

I write a note to the S's—Dr. Swammy and Mrs. Saperstone—telling them how much I appreciate all the books and that I have started a new library here in my room.

When I'm done, I seal up the envelopes and address them. In the return address spot, I write: Willa Havisham, 6 Frear Park Lane, Troy, NY 12180.

I text Tina and tell her how much I love the new clothes. I don't mention Rob. One word to Tina about a new boy and it will be all over

Bramble before breakfast.

When I come back downstairs, Mom and Sam are sitting side by side on the couch in the kitchen, legs stretched out on the table, with mugs of coffee and mounds of newspapers.

"Good morning, Willa," Mom says.

"Morning." I plop down on the couch next to them. I pick up a section of the *Times Union*, read a bit, pick up another. "Oh, my gosh," I point to a picture. "There's Mikaela, the girl I met on the beach in Bramble." The headline reads:

Congratulations to This Week's Kid of the Week
Mikaela, 9, Albany, New York

The text reads:

"This summer, Mikaela opened her own homemade ice-cream stand in her neighborhood and donated 50 percent of her profits, a total of $227.45, to the Hudson Mohawk Humane Society to purchase food and toys for the rescue cats waiting for adoption."

Kitten Mama. I laugh. "Good for you, Mikaela."

I tear out the article. I want to show this to the girls on Saturday.

"Willa," Mom says. "I have an idea."

"What?"

"We just got here, and we'll have to do some investigating to see if there's a church we like. In the meantime, we thought maybe we could start a new Sunday tradition—take a walk or a bike ride, check out some part of Troy, then find a place for breakfast."

"I like that idea. Can I show you Oakwood Cemetery today? We can bike there."

"Sounds great," Mom says.

"Let's go," Sam agrees.

I take the lead up Oakwood Avenue into the cemetery. When I reach the little gray headstone for Uncle Sam's children, I stop and wait for Mom and Sam to join me. I think about the man in the brown suit. Even if he wasn't the spirit of Uncle Sam, I decide to keep him to myself.

"I'm looking forward to the parade later," Sam says.

"Uncle Sam," Mom says, "the symbol of American patriotism. From right here in Troy, New York. That's impressive."

"And inspiring," I add.

I can't vote yet, Sam, but I have a voice, and I intend to use it.

Chapter 23
Uncle Sam Wants YOU

Change everything, except your loves.
—Voltaire

"This is the Lansingburgh part of Troy," Sam says as we drive to the parade. "Herman Melville, the author of *Moby Dick*, lived here at one point."

"*Moby Dick* was way too long a book," I say. "Melville could have used a better editor."

Sam laughs. Mom shrugs her shoulders. "You two and your books."

We park the car and make our way over to Fifth Avenue. Hundreds of people, many dressed in red, white, and blue, line the sidewalks on either side, sitting on lawn chairs and front porch steps. Kids are waving small American flags.

We plant ourselves on a clean stretch of curb near the corner of 119th Street. "We'll have to remember to bring chairs next year," Mom says, and I'm surprised to find myself nodding at her. *Just days ago, I might have snapped 'next year, Mom, really? I hope we're back home in Bramble by then.' But it's different now. I feel like I could call this place home.*

A shiny red fire truck heads our way, air horns booming, firefighters waving, the crowd cheering and waving back. I look at my parents' faces. I know they're thinking about the fire, too. The procession halts. A firefighter jumps down to the street, lifts a little girl and then a little boy up to sit in the truck, lets each of them wear a firefighter hat.

The children are better-than-meeting-Santa-Claus thrilled. It's a moment they'll never forget. Parents are taking pictures. I recall how kind the firefighters were to our family on that awful night and in the days after. One of them even came over to Nana's to see how we were doing. Another posted a billboard-sized photo of Salty Dog on his lawn. "If you see this dog call...."

I take a quick second to cross my fingers and send up a prayer for my smiling Salty Dog. *Please come home soon...*

Next up is the Fiesta Band of Mechanicville, then a group of Marine Corps veterans. People clap and salute. "Thank you for your service," someone shouts.

There's the Citizen of the Year and the Humanitarian of the Year.

A group in formal business attire processes by, smiling and waving, occasionally darting over to shake hands with people on the sidewalks. "Politicians, I bet," Mom says.

I think how uncomfortable it will be for that lady in high heels to walk the entire length of the parade route. I look down at my pink Chucks. Would anyone think less of her if she wore comfortable shoes?

Troy's Excelsior Drum and Bugle Corps is next, then the Miss Uncle Sam Pageant Winners float. Girls from toddler to teenage age, wearing crowns and gowns with sashes proclaiming their titles: Tiny Miss...Little Miss...Young Miss...Pre-Teen Miss...Teen Miss.... I recognize a few from the Oakwood Cemetery service yesterday.

"Look at that little one," Mom says, "she's got the royal wave down pat."

The Red Caps Marching Band passes by, then sheriffs, then the Veterans of Lansingburgh, followed by men carrying a black POW/MIA flag.

"Prisoner of War, Missing in Action," Sam says, in case I didn't know the acronym. He takes off his hat and puts his hand over his heart as they pass. Mom and I do the same.

More groups of Veterans pass—American Legion, Korean War Vets, Rensselaer County Veterans, U.S. Navy Seabees. I clap and wave to show respect.

The Mohonasen High School Marching Band is awesome.

I cheer for the athletes wearing Special Olympics t-shirts.

"Here comes Uncle Sam," Mom says. A thin man with long white hair and a white beard is sitting on the seat back of a blue convertible, smiling and waving energetically. He's dressed like the caricature of Uncle Sam—red and white striped hat, white stars on a blue brim, blue jacket with red and white striped lapels, white shirt with red bow tie, red and white striped pants, white gloves. He points to various people in the crowd.

"Uncle Sam wants you," people shout.

"What does that mean anyway?" I ask my parents.

"It used to mean a call to serve in the armed forces," Mom says.

"That's not the only way to serve," I say.

"Certainly not," Sam says.

There's the Uncle Sam Chorus float, men singing "O beautiful for spacious skies...," wearing stars and stripes jackets, waving to the crowd.

"I heard them singing in Oakwood Cemetery this morning. They're really good." Sam and Mom agree. As the strains of "His Truth is Marching On," wane, the unmistakable sound of bagpipes fills the air. A group in fancy kilts processes by. "I love bagpipes. Remember the man who played at Gramp's funeral?"

"It was beautiful," Mom says. "That reminds me, the high school your grandfather went to, The Doane Stuart School, is here in the Capital Region."

There's another loud fog horn, then the Speigletown Volunteer Fire Department, then the Trojan High Steppers, girls twirling batons. When the RPI Pep Band passes, they launch into "Sweet Caroline," and Mom, Sam, and I shout out the "uhn, uhn, uhn," on cue, reminding us of all the times we belted that out at Boston Red Sox games at Fenway Park. I probably should try and become a Mets or Yankees fan, but I think I'll always be a Sox girl at heart. *Not* everything *has to change.*

A group processes with a banner: "Uncle Sam Memorial Foundation, Inc.: Help us Rebuild Uncle Sam's Home in Troy." I wonder where his home was. Then a group with a Troy Public Library banner, people dressed up as a princess, Elmo, Spiderman, Thing 1 and Thing 2 from *The Cat in the Hat*. I wave to them.

"Be sure to vote 'yes' for the library budget," a lady calls out.

"That reminds me," Mom says. "We need to register."

"Yes," Sam says. "That's important."

I wish I could vote "yes" for the library budget.

"Wait until you see the Main Troy Library, Willa," Sam says. "It's downtown on Second Street, right across from Russell Sage. I know you love the Bramble library, but this is pretty spectacular."

"It looks like the parade's winding down," Mom says. "How about we show Willa your college, Sam."

"Sound okay to you, Willa?"

"Can we stop by the college library, too?"

Sam and Mom smile.

Chapter 24
Imagining Like That

The way a crow shook down on me
The dust of snow from a hemlock tree
Has given my heart a change of mood
And saved some part of a day I had rued.
　　　　　　—Robert Frost, *Dust of Snow*

"That's Sage Park on the left," Sam says, as we drive under the Welcome to Russell Sage College archway on First Street. "And Bush Memorial Center." He points to an impressive building with tall white columns, some students sitting on the steps reading and talking.

There's a long row of stately brownstones with ornate railings, interesting doors, yellow and orange mums, autumn wreaths. "Some of these are residence halls," he says.

"We saw a few," Mom adds. "They are gorgeous inside... chandeliers and marble fireplaces, carved mahogany staircases...not your average college dorm."

We park in the faculty parking lot. Carriage House, where the English faculty offices are located, is a sweet little building off a courtyard with a fountain. Sam unlocks the door, and we walk up to the second floor where he unlocks another door marked "Dr. Craig."

"You need to get a sign with your name on it, Dad." I walk straight to the bookshelves, running my fingers along Dr. Craig's many volumes of fiction.

There's a *knock, knock* and a young woman enters. "Excuse me, Professor Gracemore. I saw you and I have a question."

"*Professor Gracemore*," Mom whispers and nudges me. "I like the sound of that."

"Certainly," Sam says. "Come right in, Sarumbay. Meet my wife and my daughter, Willa. Sarumbay is in my poetry class." We smile and exchange greetings.

"I am sorry to bother you on the weekend, Professor, but can I talk with you about the mid-term project?"

"Sure thing," Sam says. "Stell, perhaps you could show Willa around campus and meet me back here in twenty?"

There's an event going on in the campus square, booths and tables set up, a band playing. Campus clubs and organizations are trying to recruit members. Mom and I stop and buy two bags of oatmeal cookies with pink frosting to support breast cancer awareness. We're both thinking of Mum and Mrs. Sivler. "I hope they're doing well," I say. Mom gives me a quick hug and we keep exploring.

"There's the president's office," Mom points. "And there's the Troy Public Library across the street. Shall we take a peek?"

"Sure." We cross over, but then I say, "Let's wait for Dad to see inside."

"Okay, let's head up the street then. The campus store is on the corner. I'd like to buy Sam a nice mug for his office. A college professor should have a suitable mug."

A woman and a little girl are walking ahead of us. The girl is carrying an armload of books. They pause in front of a gray building with two lion head sculptures. The girl thrusts her free hand into the lion's mouth, pulls it out quickly, paws her fingers in the air, and makes a roaring sound. She repeats this with the other lion.

Mom and I reach them, and the woman sees us and smiles. "It's a tradition my daughter and I have. First the library, then the lions."

The little girl looks down. "I like your pink sneakers."

"Thanks. I like that you have all those books. I like the lions, too."

"You try it," she says, books clutched to her chest. "Stick your hand in the lion's mouth, then roar. It makes you strong."

I follow her instructions.

"Now do the other lion," she says. "You get stronger every time."

Oh my gosh, I love the girls of Troy.

"Come on, Margaret," her mom says. "We need to get home now."

"She was adorable, huh?" Mom says as we keep walking. She sighs. "I did so hope you would have a little sister, Willa."

"That's okay, Mom. I'm sorry you had the miscarriage." We don't talk about it very often, but I know Mom was crushed when she lost the baby that first year with Sam.

"Thank you, Willa," she puts her arm around me. "You know, Sam and I haven't given up the idea of adoption."

"And you'd have a lot of time to spend with a new baby now." It's the closest I've come to acknowledging—and accepting—our family's changes. She smiles at me.

The campus store is called MOSS, after its founder, Margaret Olivia Slocum Sage. Mom buys a mug and a green Sage College sweatshirt. When we return to campus, Sam is standing in Lafayette Courtyard talking to another student. Popular already, of course. He introduces us to Christy from his poetry class.

"This is a beautiful campus," Mom says as we walk to our car. "The architecture, the trees. I think this is going to be a great fit, Sam."

"I think so too. The students are amazing," Sam says. "A very diverse lot, in all sorts of ways. They're from small towns, big cities, and several foreign countries. I have students from Jamaica, India, and two from Africa."

"I hope you teach them to roar, Dad. To not be afraid to stand up and speak out loudly about what they believe in." We tell him about the Troy lions.

"Not that our daughter has any shortage of bravery."

"No worries, there, Willa. I've got you and your mom for examples."

"Yes, you do," I say, and we laugh.

He looks at his phone. "I just got a text from a colleague inviting us to an impromptu pot-luck dinner tonight," Sam says. "Her name is Lori Quigley. She's Dean of the School of Education. We don't need to stay long, but I would like to make an appearance."

"Of course," Mom says.

"Sure, Dad." I know it's important for him to mingle with the faculty, especially if he wants to find a permanent teaching job here. I push away thoughts of Rob—for the moment.

We stop at Bella Napoli bakery and buy a raspberry pie. Mom would die before showing up at a party empty-handed.

*****

Dr. Quigley, "please call me Lori," and her husband, Quig, are very nice.

"Help yourself to drinks," Lori says.

"I've got the football game on if you're interested," Quig says.

I scan the room, no one my age. I join Mom and Sam in the kitchen. "Willa," Mom says, "this is Steven Bouchey, a neighbor of ours. He owns a financial planning company."

"And now a famous racehorse," a woman interjects.

"What horse is that?" Mom asks.

"Keen Ice."

"*Keen Ice*," Sam and I say together.

"He won the Travers Stakes," Sam tells Mom.

"Beat the Triple Crown winner," I say.

"I'm just one of the owners," Mr. Bouchey says. "There are about twenty of us."

Sam tells him about Mr. Belle.

"Oh, you know him?" Mr. Bouchey says. "We've been friends since college. Wonderful family."

"I believed in your horse, even though he was a long shot," I say.

"I hope you bet a lot," Mr. Bouchey says.

"Two dollars." He snaps his fingers as if to say *shucks*.

We talk with him a bit longer. He feels so bad about the Inn, but says, "We're happy to have you here in Troy. There's no place like it." He and my parents exchange numbers.

It's dark when we get back to Frear Park Lane. The Pryor's garage door is open, and I see Rob and his mom pulling out in a white Lexus. I

142

wave and they both wave back. *Keep walking, Willa.*

We're taking our time getting back to number six. Mom points out different types of architecture, and Sam comments on how old some of the houses are. The gray house set back from the street is dark, but there are lights on in the yellow house. "Do we know who lives there?" I ask.

"Gail said her name is Corinne Johnson. She's a retired teacher. Taught fourth grade. Gail said she's traveled all over the world. I believe she was in Paris just last week."

"It's late to disturb her now," Sam says, "but let's introduce ourselves tomorrow."

When I get to my room, I turn my phone on. *Beep, beep,* come the text messages from home.

Tina. Checking in to see how I'm doing: "School sucks. How are the clothes? Any hotties at your new school? We miss you!" ☹ ☹ ☹ Come home soon!" ♥ Tina

JFK: "how r u?"

I don't know how to respond to him (*I'm fine I met a cute boy last night sorry I don't hate Troy after all, how are you* seemed more than a little awkward), so I scroll down to read the rest of my messages.

Chandler: "Hope u liked the CD."

Lauren: "Did you hear Ruby's running for class president?"

Mrs. Saperstone: "Hello, Willa. How's Troy? What are you reading? Keep us posted. Dr. S and I miss you. Be sure to visit soon!"

Nana: "Got a possible lead on Salty. One of my customers saw a dog that looks like him in her neighborhood. Fingers crossed, love you SO MUCH, Nana."

Oh my God, thank you!! My throat clenches, eyes filling with tears. "Mom...Sam!" I shout, running down the stairs so fast I nearly trip. "Nana thinks they've found Salty!"

"What exactly did she say?" Mom asks.

I read her the text.

"That's encouraging," she says, "but, Willa, please don't get your hopes up too high."

"Thanks a lot, Mom."

"Willa." Sam tries to be the peacemaker, always. "Your mom doesn't want you to get hurt. Of course, we all hope for good news."

I head back up to my room, put on the Girls-Rule CD. Listening to the Katie Perry song, "Roar," I smile thinking of that little girl and the lions downtown today. I think of the Key Club girls, especially Cinderella. How quiet she is. I want to play this song for her on Saturday.

I continue reading *Off the Sidelines*. I stand the book on top of my bookshelf, right next to *I Am Malala*, covers facing out. I stare at those two strong women, continents apart, decades apart in age, each propelled by a conviction to stand up and roar about what she believes in.

What about you, Willa? What will you roar about next?

I sprawl out on my comfy window seat and look up at the stars. Same stars twinkling over Bramble tonight. Do you see the Big Dipper, Salty? Hang on buddy, Nana's coming.

In bed, I think back over these few short days in Troy, how so much has already happened. How I already feel like I belong. How I'm actually getting excited about visiting my new school tomorrow. How I can't stop thinking about Rob Pryor.

I turn on the light, open the nightstand drawer for my journal, only to remember I don't have one. I lay back in bed, smiling. *I want to write.* For years I filled all those blank books with the story of my life— the good and the bad, my hurts and hopes—destroyed in a single night.

But I'm still here and my happy's coming back. I'm excited again for the future.

I shut off the light and close my eyes, still smiling. *I feel like writing again.*

Chapter 25
Home of the Flying Horses

Truth is the only safe ground to stand on.
—Elizabeth Cady Stanton

As I get dressed to visit Troy High, I think about poor Tina and Ruby having to wear those boring Bramble Academy uniforms. Oh, how they would love showing off their fashionista flair at school every day. I choose a pair of skinny jeans, white tank and a royal blue fringed top from the "T&R Fall Collection," and lace up my pink Chucks.

I put on makeup. *What to do with my hair?* It's gotten so long. I really need a trim. Should I scrunch it into waves or hot-iron it flat? Do "the Willa" as Ruby calls it, one side straight, one side curly? Tina insisted I take her travel hair bag, complete with a blow dryer, curling iron, flat iron, diffuser, Moroccan oils, creams, gels, and hair spray.

We girls spend so much time fussing about our appearance.

I think about my Key Club girls as I run some gel through my hair. I don't want those girls to think that being pretty is the big aspiration in life. I want to encourage them to read, read, read, and work hard in school and pursue their passions. I think about how outgoing they were in speaking to me. How they tried hard to get that old city building for a clubhouse. How interested they were when I told them about Mikaela's ice-cream business. How supportive they were of each other telling me about their bracelet making, cookie baking, and dance talents. I can't wait for our meeting on Saturday.

"Troy High's only a mile from here," Sam says as we pull out of the driveway. "You can take the bus or bike."

"Or even run, I did that yesterday morning."

My parents look at each other and smile.

"The Home of the Flying Horses," I say when we arrive.

We walk up one, two, three flights of stairs.

For such a big school, inside it's surprisingly quiet; only a few teachers and students milling about. A man in a suit approaches us with a smile. "May I help you?"

"We have an appointment to register our daughter, Willa Havisham," Mom says. "I'm Estelle Clancy. This is my husband, Sam Gracemore."

"I'm Ian McShane, a vice principal." He shakes our hands. "Welcome to Troy High."

He shows us where to sign the visitor's log and get passes. "Oh, Mrs. Hannan," he says, to a lady in the hall, "meet Willa Havisham and her parents. Would you mind escorting them to the guidance office? Charlie Riccio's expecting them."

"Certainly," Mrs. Hannan says with a friendly smile. "Welcome to Troy High, Willa. You're going to love it. My three children all graduated from here, and I met some of my best friends in the world in this place. I'm retired now, but we still get together all the time."

Mrs. Hannan introduces us to Mr. Riccio in the guidance office.

"I've reviewed your transcripts from Bramble Academy, Willa. Quite an outstanding record." He smiles. "You must be so proud of your daughter," he says to Mom and Sam.

"We are," Sam says. My mom smiles.

"If you'd like," Mr. Riccio says, looking over my file again, "based on this, we could test Willa right through to eleventh grade. We have lots of juniors taking college credit courses."

"No," Mom says. "We want Willa to enjoy her teenage years. She'll be in college soon enough." She looks at me to make sure I concur.

I nod in agreement.

"All right then," Mr. Riccio says. "I'm sure Willa will be happy and challenged in these classes." He hands me a schedule. "Global History, Honors English, Accelerated Math, Living Environment, French Three, and Gym. You'll just need to choose an elective. The arts are a huge strength of ours. Chorus, Band, Drama…"

"Drama," I say, and Mom smiles at me encouragingly.

"Excellent," Mr. Riccio says. "Will you want to continue with soccer, Willa?"

"I don't think so, but definitely track."

"You can join cross-country now," Mr. Riccio says. "Then indoor track and field in the winter and track in the spring."

"Willa's quite the runner," Mom says.

"I run like a girl." All three turn and look at me. Sam smiles at me and winks. "I'm fast," I explain.

"Excellent," Mr. Riccio says. "Okay, now then, you can start classes as early as tomorrow, but if you're still settling in, perhaps you'd like to wait until Monday."

"I think I'd like to wait 'til Monday." I look over to Sam and Mom for approval and they both nod.

"Oh, good," Mr. Riccio says, looking up as a girl pops her head into the office. "Alaina-Grace," he says, "would you please come in? I want you to meet our new student."

Alaina-Grace looks my age. She smiles, friendly. I smile back. Mr. Riccio introduces us. "Willa will be in most of your classes, Alaina. I'd like for you to look out for her, help her navigate the cafeteria…"

The way he says "navigate" makes me a little nervous. Sam winks at me.

"Can Willa sit in on a class today?" Mom asks.

"Certainly," Mr. Riccio says. "First period started." He checks a schedule. "Alaina, please take Willa to Mr. Hayes's room. It's an eleventh-grade English class, but it will give you a good sense of things. And then at eight-fifty, take her next door to Mrs. Tompkins' room." To me he says, "It's the Advanced Algebra class you'll actually be joining. I'll buzz both teachers to let them know you're coming."

"We'll meet you back at the main entrance," Sam says. "Have fun."

I take a deep breath and walk with Alaina-Grace.

"You'll love Mrs. Tompkins," she says as we start down the hall. "She's everybody's favorite math teacher. Mr. Hayes is cool, too. He's an author."

"What's our class reading in English right now?"

"*Whirligig.*" I haven't read it, which is a relief. I like discovering new stories along with my classmates. I tell Alaina this and she laughs. "Oh yeah, you'll get along in Hayes' class just fine." Alaina knocks on the classroom door and we enter.

Everyone stares.

"Welcome," Mr. Hayes says. "Have a seat wherever." He turns to the class. "Willa is a new student."

"*N----iiiiice,*" says a boy, in an appreciative tone. There's laughter.

"She's a *sophomore,*" Mr. Hayes says.

"Like that matters," a girl says, and people laugh.

We sit by the window. I count twenty-five students. That was the size of my entire grade level at Bramble Academy. About half of the class is black. There were only three students of color in the entire Bramble Academy—none in my class, none in my neighborhood either. I think of Rob.

Mr. Hayes resumes teaching, sitting comfortably on a desktop. He has his students' attention and respect. He's giving a quiz—four questions and a bonus.

"Does it have to be complete sentences?" the boy who was flirting with me calls out.

There are posters around the room—Toni Morrison, Ralph Ellison, Sherman Alexi, Richard Wright, the Beatles, Woodstock 1969, *Water for Elephants*, President Obama's "This is Our Moment," and one for Mr. Hayes' book, *The Trouble with Lemons*. I wonder what it's about.

"Yes, Tyler, I want complete sentences. The bonus question is a corny joke," Mr. Hayes is saying. "It's worth five points."

"We should go next door to math now," Alaina-Grace whispers, and we quietly get up.

"Where are you going?" flirty boy asks, and his friends laugh. Alaina glares at him and pulls me out of the classroom.

Mrs. Tompkins greets us with a warm smile. She points to some open seats then turns back to her class. "How did you arrive at that?" she asks a student, and the girl explains her calculations.

Later, at the sound of the buzzer, Mrs. Tompkins calls out some students' names. "Amanda, Ria, Sydney, Hannah, Chelsea, Meghan, would you please stay for a second?"

Mrs. Tompkins puts her hand on my shoulder. "Girls, this is Willa. She's new to Troy High. I'd appreciate it if you'd make her feel welcome."

"Sure," Chelsea says.

"You're in time for Homecoming," Amanda says, excitedly.

"There's the football game on Friday," Ria says, "then the dance on Saturday."

"Who goes to the dance?" I ask.

"Everybody," Sydney says.

"It's for all four years," Meghan adds. "A lot of people go."

"You don't need a date," Chelsea says. "People go with friends. It's more fun that way, anyway."

"When is Homecoming?" I ask.

"The game's on Friday, the twenty-fifth," Hannah says. "The dance is the next night."

"What do you wear?" I ask. *Tina would be proud.*

"It's semi-formal," Amanda says, "most girls wear short dresses." She pulls out her phone, looking at Mrs. Thompson for approval. "This is what we wore last year." She brings up a picture of a group of girls, all in fancy dresses, making silly faces at the camera.

"We had so much fun last year. You should definitely come." I tell them I'll try. *Making new friends might not be so hard.*

When Alaina-Grace and I exit the classroom into the hallway, it's as busy as Times Square—hundreds of students passing by in pairs and packs, laughing, shouting, opening and slamming locker doors.

"Hey, Aisey. Hi, Kaelyn," Alaina-Grace calls out to friends.

"How many kids are in this school?" I ask.

"Eleven hundred, twelve hundred, something like that." Alaina-Grace does her best to stick by me in the hallway crowd. "But there are only 300 sophomores."

"Only 300!"

Alaina laughs. "Don't worry, you'll be fine. Come on." She grabs my hand. "I'll get you back to your parents."

Chapter 26
The Capacity to Vote

Change will not come if we wait for some other person or some other time. We are the ones we've been waiting for. We are the change that we seek.
—Barack Obama

Alaina Grace and I exchange numbers. "Call me anytime, okay?" she says. "I'll be looking for you next week." And then she's off in a sea of strangers who hopefully will soon be friends.

Mom and Sam are waiting for me in the lobby with smiles and hopeful expressions. "So what do you think?" Mom asks.

"I think I'm going to like it. It's a bit bigger than I'm used to..." I trail off, still intimidated by the sheer number of students moving through the halls at that moment.

"It will certainly be an adjustment, after Bramble Academy, but there are a lot of benefits to going to a big school. I had over five-hundred students in my senior class," Sam tells me. My eyes widen. "You'll be fine!" Sam gives me a reassuring hug.

"You seem to be getting along with that Alaina girl fine," Mom reminds me. "All you need is one or two friends, and it gets much easier." She hands me a Troy High assignment notebook. There's a white horse with wings on a tall purple "T."

"That's Pegasus," Sam says, "the immortal winged horse that sprang forth from Medusa's neck when she was beheaded by Perseus."

"Lovely," Mom says. She checks the time. "I need to get home. My friend Penny is picking me up soon."

"And I have to get to class," Sam says. "I read that this is Troy Restaurant Week. Shall we have dinner downtown tonight?"

"Sounds good," Mom says.

"Fine by me," I say. Sam drives us home.

*****

When we get home, Mom's friend Penny has just pulled up in the driveway. We get out and Mom introduces us. Penny is a whirlwind of nostalgia and excitement, making all sorts of references to memories she shares with Mom. "Are you sure you won't join us, Willa? I'm taking your mom to the Whistling Kettle on Broadway. It's one of my favorite places."

"Thanks anyway," I say. "You two have fun."

For lunch, I make a tuna sandwich and then sit on the couch and look out at the birdfeeder. I make a cup of lemon tea and take it up to my room. I grab a bag of candy and *Off the Sidelines* and sprawl out on my window-seat cushion.

It's appalling some of the things Kristen Gillibrand had to deal with because she's a woman. When she became senator in 2009, a union leader told her to lose weight. "When I first met you in 2006, you were beautiful," he said, "a breath of fresh air. To win…you need to be beautiful again."

A male colleague in Congress said, "You're even pretty when you're fat." Another told her to exercise so she wouldn't "get too porky." After having a baby, a guy squeezed her stomach and said, "I like my girls chubby."

Unbelievable! She's a *United States senator*. I bet stuff like that wouldn't happen if there were more women in Congress.

Maybe I'll run for office someday. Of course, it would help if I could vote first. I Google "voting age" and find a map showing legal voting ages throughout the world. At sixteen, you can vote in Argentina, Austria, Brazil, Cuba, Ecuador, Nicaragua, and three self-governing British Crown dependencies—the Isle of Man, Jersey, and Guernsey.

Wikipedia says, "The vast majority of countries in the world have established a voting age. Most governments consider that those younger than the chosen threshold lack the capacity to decide how to cast a vote."

WHAT? "Lack the capacity?" That's insulting.

I read on. Before the Second World War, almost all countries had voting ages of twenty-one or higher. In the 1970's, several Western European countries lowered the age to eighteen, starting with the United Kingdom in 1970. The United States, Canada, France and Australia followed soon afterward. By the end of the twentieth century, most countries had adopted eighteen as the legal voting age. If young men could be drafted into war at eighteen, they should be able to vote, too.

What a concept.

Brazil lowered its minimum voting age to sixteen in 1988. Austria did so in 2007. You can vote at sixteen in Bosnia, Herzegovina, Croatia, and Slovenia if you are employed. *What about America?* This is so interesting. I read on and on.

In the 2000's there were several legislative proposals to make sixteen the legal voting age in various U.S. states, including California, Florida, and Alaska, but none were successful. *What about Massachusetts? What about New York?* I wonder what Senator Gillibrand thinks.

When Mom gets home, I march downstairs to her office to talk about these things.

"I think it's wonderful that you are questioning all of this Willa. Half of the country's eligible voters didn't even vote in the last presidential election. If smart, informed teenagers want to vote, I certainly think you should have that right."

"I don't think I'm the only teenager who would want to vote. We could really make a difference."

"I love the way you're thinking," Mom says. "I just made coffee, want a cup?"

"Sure, thanks." I usually drink tea, but it doesn't matter. I follow her into the kitchen.

A wave of emotion comes over me. My mom is making time for me. My mom and I are hanging out together talking, just the two of us. And it feels like she's on my side. Talking with me like an adult and respecting my opinion. Letting me be exactly myself.

"Want some?" She slides the sugar bowl my way. I take a sip of the coffee. "Yes, please."

Chapter 27
New People, New Places

We hold these truths to be self-evident: that all men and women are created equal.

—Elizabeth Cady Stanton

When I come downstairs ready to leave for dinner downtown, I see through the window that Mom and Sam are sitting out on the front porch. "Penny introduced me to some other friends," I overhear her telling him. Her voice is higher, bouncier than I'm used to. *She's excited. And happy.* "They want me to join them tomorrow at this networking luncheon for women in business, sponsored by the Chamber of Commerce. I can't believe it, Sam, but I'm a little nervous…"

I walk onto the porch and find them hugging. Mom's head is resting on Sam's shoulder, eyes closed, smiling like she wouldn't want to be anywhere but right there in his arms. I quietly turn around, not wanting to interrupt something so special, but Sam catches me.

"Hey, Willa," Sam says. He motions for me to sit down next to him, and he puts his other arm around me.

Mom smiles at me. *Home is where the heart is.* Maybe the reason Troy has been growing on me is that I brought my heart with me. I smile back at her, full to the brim with happiness. "Oh, I almost forgot, this is for the car." I pull the "Enjoy Troy" sticker out of my pocket and hand it to Sam.

"I think I will," Sam says after he reads it.

"Me, too," Mom says.

"Me, three."

Mom locks eyes with me, pursing her lips like she's fighting back tears. "Thank you, Willa. Thank you for giving this a chance. I know this isn't what you wanted."

"We're a family," I say. "This is good for our family."

She hugs me.

"Change is good for the soul," I say.

My mom laughs, blows her nose. "You and Sam and your quotes. Who said that?"

"Me."

*****

It's hard to choose a restaurant, so many of them sound good. We decide on the Ilium Café on Broadway, where we are seated at an outdoor table overlooking Monument Square. There's a towering statue of a woman blasting a trumpet in the center. I think of the woman who gave me the keys that day. Could that have been…?

"What looks good, Willa?" Mom says, peering at the menu.

Sam orders the fresh-seared Ahi Tuna with wild-pear-and-broccoli coleslaw. Mom and I opt for the curried chicken salad on croissants with homemade potato chips.

Sam points to the building across the street, the Charles A. Lucas Confectionery. "Is that a candy store?"

"No, a really fun bar and interesting restaurant," Mom says. "Penny raved about it. The owners, a young couple, Heather Lavine and Vic Christopher, are the new royalty in Troy. They have an outdoor atrium and on Sunday afternoons host a 'Yappy Hour.' People bring their dogs. Isn't that cute? *Yappy Hour.*"

As soon as she says it, Mom realizes her mistake. "Oh, Willa, I'm sorry." She touches my hand. "I'm sure we'll hear good news about Salty soon."

"I hope so," I squeeze her hand back and change the subject. "I read an article about that couple. Mr. Christopher was talking about how affordable it is to renovate buildings in Troy compared to Brooklyn where they're from. He talked about how creative people can be when they have space to do 'cool stuff.'" I think of my Key Club girls. I tell Mom about how they wanted to get that building for a clubhouse. "I said I would try and help them. We're going to meet on Saturdays. I'm bringing books and

156

candy."

"Of course you are," Mom says with a knowing smile. "That's my girl, always finding ways to pay her community rent. Is there a way we can help?"

"I'm good for now, but I'll let you know. Thanks."

My mom tells the waitress, Sarah, that we're new in Troy. "I just moved here a few months ago," Sarah says. "I do pottery. The arts community in this city is amazing." She points across the square. "That's the Arts Center of the Capital Region over there. My boyfriend's teaching a digital photography class right now."

A lady at the table next to us overhears this and leans over. "Be sure to check out Troy Night Out. It's the last Friday night of every month. There's live music, art shows, fun stuff to do all over downtown."

"Thank you," Mom says, checking her phone. "So that's Friday, September twenty-fifth." She types it in. "Let's do that," she says to Sam and me.

"I already have plans. It's Homecoming Weekend at school. There's a football game Friday night and a dance on Saturday." I still need to ask Rob.

"A dance?" my mom says, slyly.

"People go with friends," I say quickly. "I'll probably go with Alaina-Grace."

"That is great! I'm so happy you're already making friends." Mom seems pacified, for now. "Let me know if you want to shop for a dress."

"I hear football is really big at Troy High," Sam says and takes a bite of food.

"Maybe we'll go with you to the game," Mom suggests. "Meet some of these new friends of yours?"

"No, no, I'm sure you'll meet them, eventually. You two go to Troy Night Out and find out what it's like. It'll be fun." They're not convinced, so I try another tactic. "How are your classes going, Dad?"

*****

After dinner, we walk past a women's clothing store, Truly Rhe, bright and colorful fashions in the window. "Do you mind?" Mom asks, and Sam and I follow her into the store.

"Hello," calls a pretty lady wearing a brocade jacket and a velvet hat. She looks very chic, very Cosmopolitan or European or something. "Welcome. I'm Rhe."

"Oh, so this is your store? It's beautiful." Mom runs her hand across a rack of jackets.

"Thank you," the woman nods. "Have fun looking around, and let me know if I can help."

"You take your time, babe," Sam says. "How about we meet you in Riverfront Park in twenty minutes or so."

Mom lifts a blouse off a rack. "Oh, I love this." She looks at Sam.

"Okay, how about a half hour then?" Sam laughs.

Sam and I go to the Arts Center, check out the exhibit, pick up brochures. "Look at these writing classes, Dad. Maybe you want to teach here, too?" He takes a couple and looks down at me.

"This is a nice change of pace, you trying to find me more jobs in Troy."

I pretend not to know what what he's talking about. "It smells beautiful in here," I say to the woman at the front desk.

"It's the shop next door," she says. "All handcrafted soaps and lotions."

Sam and I stop at Dante's for a dish of frozen yogurt. "We never should have left Mom alone in that store," I tell him as I scoop Heath Bar crunch bits on top of my yogurt.

"Do you think we need to send in a search party?"

"Maybe not quite yet." We head back out to the street. We pause to look in the window of Market Block Books, the yogurt the only thing preventing us from going inside. My Dad and I can never resist a bookstore.

We find a nice spot to sit and wait for Mom in Riverfront Park.

When she joins us, she's carrying a big bag from Market Block Books in addition to her clothing purchases.

"What did you buy?" I ask.

"Just some gifts," she says.

I tell them about the lady in the blue dress and the trumpet and the keys. "We were right over there," I point. "She was..." I still can't quite find the words to describe her. "...different. But in a good way. And she was so excited to welcome me to Troy."

"Be sure to keep your guard up, Willa," Mom cautions. This isn't Bramble. It's a city. You need to be careful. Not everyone is as innocent as they appear."

I look at Sam. We smile. Sam and I trust the world a bit more.

Several boats are docked at the marina along with a larger ship, the *J.P. Morgan*. My mom takes a brochure from a nearby rack. "They're doing a Halloween DJ cruise."

"Sounds fun," Sam says. "Maybe the Pryors would like to join us."

"Do you know how to do the Cupid Shuffle, Mom?"

"Sort of. I should know from all the weddings."

"Practice it on YouTube. Rob's mom is really into dancing."

We head back to the car. "It is such a beautiful night," Sam says. "It's supposed to be nice all week. Aren't you glad that you have a few more days to play hooky before you start school again?"

"I plan on taking full advantage of it." I'm thinking of the exploring and the club planning I can get done in the next few days.

"That's my girl." My mom's phone beeps. She checks the screen. "Hold up," she says, stopping. She types something back. It takes her awhile.

"Everything okay?" Sam asks.

"Yes. Penny is inviting me *to another* event. She's on the board of the YWCA, and they're having a program honoring 'resourceful women' in the area. The Y helps women in crisis situations with affordable housing, counseling, childcare, help getting jobs..."

"Sounds like Penny's paying her community rent," Sam says.

· Mom's phone beeps again. She reads it and laughs. "Now she's telling me about a 'Fuel Her Fire' event sponsored by Girls Incorporated. Penny's on the board there, too. Michelle Obama is Honorary National Chair. The want to empower girls to be strong, smart, and bold."

"Sounds like that's right up your alley, Willa," Sam says.

"Can I go with you, Mom?"

"Absolutely. I'll order tickets right now."

When we get home, I head up to my room. There's a text from Rob asking if I want to go out for ice cream tomorrow night.

Sounds great, what time?

Later, I go downstairs to brew a cup of chamomile tea, and when I come back up, there are two things propped against my door, wrapped in pretty paper with the Market Block Books' seal. My mom bought me books?

I sit in my window seat. The setting sun casts a golden glow over the hills of Frear Park. I open the first package. *A Short Course in American HERstory*. I flip it over, reading the back: "A short and concise overview of American feminism, *HERstory* is a must for any young readers looking to learn about the women traditional history books leave behind." It goes on to list some of the women the book covers: Susan B. Anthony, Elizabeth Cady Stanton, Sojourner Truth, Lucretia Mott, Lucy Stone, Harriet Tubman, Dorothea Dix, Carrie Chapman Catt, Elizabeth Blackwell.... Some names are familiar, most are not. I can't wait to read this.

I tear back the paper from the second gift. A bright pink blank book with "Carpe That Diem" embossed in gold on the cover. Inside there is a handwritten message from Mom:

> *Dear Willa,*
> *Change happens, love heals,*
> *follow your compass,*
> *write your truth always*
> *run like a girl, smart with heart,*

and roar until they listen.
Love always,
Mom

I laugh and then cry and then hurry to my desk. I turn on the light, and open to that first blank, beautiful, anything-is-possible page. I write about the fire, and Salty, and having to leave Bramble and all the people I love. I write about Rob…. I write about Troy…how in a matter of days, its people, places, and possibly ghosts have welcomed me and lured me in. I write about the Key Club girls and how I want to help them get that building because "people need space to do cool stuff." I write about *I Am Malala* and *Off the Sidelines* and how teenagers should be able to vote and how we need a better phrase than "hi guys," and how someday, maybe, I'll run for office.

I open a saltwater taffy and pop it in. Mmmm. Cinnamon.

Last week I was into wedding planning; now I'm thinking about politics. *Change happens, love heals.* She gets me after all.

I walk downstairs and find her in her office, just getting off the phone. I move toward her and give her a hug. "Thank you for the presents, Mom."

"I love you, Willa."

"Love you more."

Chapter 28
Street Glass

I was born by the river
In a little tent
And just like the river
I've been running ever since
It's been a long, a long time coming
But I know a change gonna come.
—Sam Cooke, "A Change Is Gonna Come"

Which way to run this morning? I look up and down the street and decide to go in a new direction. I run down Middleburgh Avenue. There's an elementary school on the corner. I turn left and run past it. There's a purple banner with "Welcome to School 2," in bright orange block letters. There are colorful murals on the parking lot wall and cheery sunflowers all along the fence. It looks like such a fun place to learn! I keep going, wondering if that's where Cinderella and friends go to school.

Turning right onto Rensselaer Street, the side of the brick building on the corner catches my eye. On it, someone painted a large white square, like a sheet of paper, then several sentences in black. I jog in place to read them. One line, in particular, calls out to me:

"If nothing changes, nothing changes."

Huh. I'd never thought of it that way, but it's true. If nothing had ever changed, Stella would never have met Sam; Nana would never have opened Sweet Bramble Books; my half-brother Will would never have visited; the S's would never have gotten married. All the beautiful moments in my life, those that fill me right to the top with joy, they were changes. And all the things Mom and I have been talking about, things like teenagers getting to vote, and putting more women in office—those are changes. And the leaders in the book that Mom gave me last night, women like Elizabeth Cady Stanton and Sojourner Truth, they were pushing for *big* changes in their times. I mentally shoot a note to the anonymous artist, thanking him or her for reminding me that *If nothing changes, nothing changes.*

I continue on my way, eyes on the sidewalk, still getting used to city running, the uneven pavement, the ups and downs of curbs. Small bits of litter catch the sunlight— candy and gum wrappers, scratched off lottery tickets, a piece of green glass. I pick it up. The edges have smoothed over time. I think of all the beach glass I've collected in my life.

This isn't sea glass; this is *street glass.* Different, yet the same color green. I stick it in my pocket and head home.

Sam is upstairs in his office writing. I tell him about the building with the sentences painted on the side. "Sounds like an urban poet to me," he says.

"Are you working on a poem, Dad?" I try to peek over his shoulder.

"No, not quite yet. I'm trying to remember the quotes." He moves his hands so I can see the pages, filled with different quotes from the Bramble Board.

The first time I saw Sam, he was putting a quote up on a board outside his house. He had a book filled with inspirational quotes collected over the years. He and I used them for our Bramble Board. "Your mom bought me this blank book at Market Block and in light of all that our family has been going through, I thought I'd look up some thoughts on *change.*"

"Mom's on a roll with perfect presents this week." I read some of the quotes out loud, trying to get a better feel for them:

> *You must change your life.*
> —Rainer Maria Rilke

> *Progress is impossible without change, and those who cannot change their minds cannot change anything.*
> —George Bernard Shaw

It's time for us as a people to start makin' some changes.
Let's change the way we eat, let's change the way we live,
And let's change the way we treat each other.
　　　　　　　　—Tupac Shakur, "Changes"

Never change when love has found its home.
　　　　　　—Sextus Propertius, c. 54 BCE – 2 BCE

"Sextus Propertius. Who's he?"

Sam looks up at me. "No idea."

We laugh and he points out a different quote. "I like this one:

The greatest discovery of all time is that a person can
change his future by merely changing his attitude.
　　　　　　　　　—Oprah Winfrey

"With all due respect to Oprah," I say, "and she is one of the most inspirational people on the planet, why didn't she say '*his or her* future' or '*one's* future' so we're all included equally?"

Sam smiles. "Why don't you write and ask her?"

"Maybe," I say. "Oh, and, let's add that urban poet's quote about change to the book."

*****

I'm reading *My Name is Mina* by David Almond. I underline this passage:

"Maybe writing's like walking… you set off writing like you set off walkingand you don't really need to know where you're going till you get there,and you don't know what you'll pass along the way…writing's like taking some words for a walk."

Writing's like taking some words for a walk? I love that. And I think I'm ready to take some of my words for a long-overdue walk.

After breakfast, I've curled up in my window seat, still stumped on a particular question: What book to choose for Saturday's meeting?

I call Market Block Books. Stanley answers. I tell him what I'm looking for.

"*Sunny Holiday* would be good. Sunny's a fourth-grade girl, a poet and budding politician who calls out the town mayor on why he hasn't kept his promise to build that new playground and fix the town pool. I have two copies. Could that hold you over for now? I can order more; they'll be in soon."

"That would be great, thanks. And put aside three journals for me, too. Any colors are fine, just make sure they're all different." I want the girls to have something that is uniquely their own.

I look out my window. My peaceful morning has been disturbed as usual by that annoying golf-course lawnmower guy, but the sound is getting fainter now. I watch as he makes his way over to a red brick building far down in the corner. I notice a chimney, pretty fancy for a shed to store lawnmowers in. Could that be the building the girls were talking about?

I lace up my Chucks and go to investigate.

"Excuse me," I say, to a man wearing a City of Troy shirt. "Is this the building that's going to be a clubhouse for golfers?"

"Yep. All of Parks and Rec is being consolidated up on Frear Avenue."

I look inside the building. Hardwood floors, two Hearthstone fireplaces, tiled murals on the walls, lovely windows…. I hurry home and type up my thoughts.

I Google "Troy mayor." His name is Patrick Madden, and the Deputy Mayor is Monica Kurzejeski. I put on a nice top and jeans, get on my bike and go.

It's time to do some roaring.

Chapter 29
Meeting with the Mayor

*Cautious, careful people, always casting about to
preserve their reputation and social standing, never
can bring about a reform. Those who are really in
earnest must be willing to be anything or nothing in the
world's estimation.*

—Susan B. Anthony

City Hall is on River Street, not too far. I barely notice the ride over, I'm
so pumped up. I lock up my bike and scan the directory. The mayor's
office is on the third floor. I take the elevator up and go over my plan. I'm
going to go in and, respectfully, introduce myself and ask the secretary
for ten minutes of the mayor's time. "No, I don't have an appointment," I
say out loud to the empty elevator. "But I come on behalf of a wonderful
group of Troy girls who have an excellent proposal for the city." The doors
open and I walk into his office, confident that I've perfected my best roar.

She smiles when she hears my introduction. "Good for you. I'm
sorry, though, the mayor is booked all day today and then is going out of
town. I can put you down for next Tuesday, say three p.m."

"That's too late," I start to say, but then I think for a minute. The
girls would be able to come with me if we met then. I really want to give
them a chance to talk to the mayor themselves—that's the best way to
show them how to roar like girls. "Could we do three-thirty? I would like
to bring the girls so they can present their plan themselves."

She nods. "Let me see what I can do. Just a moment." She goes to
a large computer screen and clicks around for a few minutes. "What name
should I put the appointment under?"

"The Key Club Girls," I tell her proudly.

"Oh, that's a lovely name." She gives me a thick business card with
"Key Club Girls" and our meeting time written in flawless handwriting.
"Makes me think about … I don't know, opening doors to the future,

doors of opportunity, things like that. I wish I'd had a club like that when I was young."

"They need a place to gather," I say. "People need space to do cool stuff."

The phone beeps. "I have to take this, Willa. We will see you and your girls back here, next Tuesday, all right?" She gives me an encouraging smile. "I know the mayor will be eager to hear their proposal."

"We'll be there." I leave the office grinning.

I bike home much slower, taking the time to soak in sights I've already seen, feeling them start to become familiar. A few days ago, I didn't want to be here. I closed myself off to the city and change and all the possibilities it could bring with it. Those girls helped me open up. Well, them and... "*Welcome to the grand Greek city of...*" I don't care if she's a character or a spirit or an exceptionally kind person. She welcomed me with such pomp and genuine warmth; her kindness shocked me right out of my anger. "*Allow me to present you with the keys to the city...*" *They're going to be the keys of that and so much more, in the hands of the Key Club Girls.*

*****

I'm excited to tell Mom about the mayor's office, but she's in the shower when I get home. Later she knocks on my door. I'm working on a Girl's Roar Playlist for our club meeting on Saturday.

"Come in!"

Mom listens to the Alicia Keys song "Girl On Fire" and starts swaying to the music. "I love this song," she says. "Alicia Keys – now there's a woman who knows how to roar."

"I want to play songs for the Club about being strong and proud to be a girl."

"What do you have so far?"

I read her my list: Kelly Clarkson's "Stronger"...Beyoncé's "Run

the World (Girls)" and "Pretty Hurts"…Taylor Swift's "Fearless"…
Martina McBride's "This One's for the Girls"…Pink's "Perfect"…Christina
Aguilera's "Beautiful"…Colbie Caillat's "Try"….

"How about some old school?" Mom says. "Aretha Franklin's
'R-E-S-P-E-C-T' and, of course, Whitney Houston's 'Greatest Love of All.'"

"How's that go again?"

Mom sings a few lines for me. "I believe the children are our
future, teach them well and let them lead the way, show them all the
beauty they possess inside…Give them a sense of pride."

My mom has such a pretty voice: sweet, high, and clear.
Sometimes at BUC on Sunday mornings, I'd be standing next to her and
close my eyes and listen. "Perfect. I'll add that, too."

"Tell me more about these girls." My mom sits on my bed and
listens with great interest.

I tell her all about them. How they made the whirligigs for the
park. And how the girls are all so different, but they seem so close. "They
were so supportive of each other, telling me about their different talents
and hobbies. I really feel a connection with them."

"That is because you are a wonderful, kindhearted young woman
who pays attention to the people around her and knows how to roar when
she needs to. Sounds like you're going to roar like a lion for these girls."

"Not roar like a lion, roar like a girl. Like you said, 'smart with
heart,' and loudly so people can hear."

My mom smiles and shakes her head. "I can see it now. All of the
interviews I'll be doing—David Muir…Steve Harvey…Ellen DeGeneres…
CNN…Oprah…"

"Mom, what are you talking about?"

"They'll all want to meet the mom of the youngest woman to run
for president."

"*President!?*"

"Well, maybe you'll start with senator." .

"*Senator!?*"

"All right then, governor."

"Mom. I'm fifteen. I can't even vote yet."

"Actually, you're still fourteen. Okay, then. Start with mayor."

"I didn't even tell you the best part!" I fill her in on my visit to the mayor's office. "And the timing is good because the girls can practice their presentation on Saturday."

"The mayor sounds like a good man," she says as she stands up and walks to my bookcase. "I see you're starting a new library. My daughter, the bibliophile. I'll make sure to mention that in the interviews," she says with a wink.

I spend a few minutes finding the songs she suggested. When I finally look back up, I see my mom wrap her arms around herself and shudder.

"Mom. What's wrong?"

"I'm a little nervous about getting back in the game. I'm excited about going to that Chamber event, meeting new people, but I don't even have business cards."

"Make some up on the computer. It's easy. I'll show you."

"Thank you. I know how. It's just…what do I print on them? I don't have a business anymore."

I walk over and stand beside my mom. "Mom…write 'Stella Clancy, Six Frear Park Lane, Troy,' and your email address, then leave the rest blank. You're starting a fresh new chapter in your life. That's exciting, Mom."

"Exciting and unnerving. I used to be a fairly famous wedding planner, now—"

"That's *one thing* you were," I interrupt. "You also ran a successful inn, you're awesome at renovating old buildings and interior design, and you're a great mom, wife, daughter, friend, runner, role model—"

"Role model to whom?"

"Me!" I put my hands on her shoulders and turn her to face me. "Where do you think I get all of this girl-power strength from?"

"Thank you, Willa. I appreciate that."

"I appreciate you, Mom."

"You'll be a great role model to those girls, Willa."

"There's a lot they can teach me, too. Plus, we're going to have fun!"

"That's another good song. Cyndi Lauper's 'Girls Just Want to Have Fun.'"

"Well, that's not all we want."

We laugh.

"Okay now," I push my mom toward the door. "Go pick out a power outfit for tomorrow and print out some business cards. You are the strong, smart, and bold Stella Clancy, and when people ask what you do, tell them you have an MBA with honors from New York University, and that you are an entrepreneur who's considering how to make her next mark on the world. Don't be shy. Be exactly yourself. Roar like a girl. Dad and I are so proud of you."

Chapter 30
The Snowman

*I think the girl who is able to earn her own living
and pay her own way should be as happy as anybody on
earth. The sense of independence and security is very sweet*
—Susan B. Anthony

In all the excitement, I'd almost forgotten about my date with Rob. *Almost* but not quite. I lace up my pink sneakers and smile at the happy girl in the mirror. *Be exactly yourself*, I mouth to my reflection before I head out the door.

Rob pulls into our driveway at 7:00 p.m., in a bright-orange sports car with a very loud motor.

"It's my dad's. A sixty-three Karmann Ghia."

"Like in that movie *Sixteen Candles*," Mom says, coming up behind us with Sam. Sam looks in the window, admiring the seats and dashboard and control panel.

"My father is huge into cars," Rob says. "He builds remote control cars and planes, drones too."

"I know," Sam says, "he showed me some when we were at your house for dinner."

"He's got a pretty sick man cave, huh?" Rob says, laughing.

"Yes," Sam says. He looks at my mom. "I think I need one of those." Stella mouths *no* and Sam hangs his head in mock despair.

"Are you planning on building drones?" she asks.

"Perhaps," Sam says.

"And pilot it where exactly?" I ask.

"What happens in the man cave, stays in the man cave." Rob holds out his fist, and he and Sam do the power bump.

"I like your parents," Rob says as we pull away. "My folks do, too."

"Thanks. We like your family as well. Josie's a hoot."

"Josie's something, all right."

People turn to look at the car as we drive up Fifth Avenue through what is probably a usually quiet residential neighborhood. Not tonight, though; not with Rob and the Ghia driving through. An older man waves, another gives us a thumb's up.

"People love this car," Rob says.

I love how small the interior is; we're seated so close together. Watching Rob's right hand adjusting the gears, I resist the urge to put my hand on his.

Sadly, it's only a short car ride to the ice-cream shop. Rob carefully parks, double and triple checking every mirror. "I'm my dad's favorite son right now. I don't know if that would still be true if I chipped the paint on his baby."

"You're the *only* son." I slide out of the car.

"My point exactly."

There's a smiling snowman in red earmuffs and scarf on top of the ice cream place. People are sitting at picnic tables, waiting in line.

We keep up a steady stream of banter as we walk into the shop.

It takes us awhile to get to the front of the line, but I don't mind because we're having so much fun. He tells me stories about growing up in Troy, about what it's been like growing up with two sisters. He talks about summers they spent with his grandparents down in the south and visits to New York. "Mom loves the restaurants, Dad loves the museums, and Josie loves those darn Broadway shows."

"And what about you? What do you love?"

He takes a second to think like he's almost surprised at being asked. We've finally gotten our ice cream (me, coffee; him, butter pecan), and he steers me toward the only open table. "I like the city itself. I know it's a cliché, but New York really does *feel* different than anywhere else. There's an energy around the city…going there feels like recharging."

I take a big spoonful of ice cream. "My mom has always said that, too. She got her MBA there." I think carefully, trying to make sense of what I want to say about Stella. "I don't think she ever really liked living in Bramble. I mean, she loved the Inn and her business, and I know she loved that Sam and I were so happy in Bramble. But I think Mom's heart has always been in the city."

"I'm sorry about everything that happened to make you move, but I can't be sorry that you're in Troy now." He smiles and reaches across the table. My heart jumps when he laces his fingers with mine. "I'm very very not sorry."

*****

Sooner than I'd like, we head back home. We're turning onto Frear Park Lane, and I'm about to ask him about the Homecoming Dance, when I see it. Nana's old Volvo station wagon in my driveway.

This is about to be the best night or worst night ever.

Chapter 31
Pumpkin Pie

Nature never repeats herself, and the possibilities
of one human soul will never be found in another.
—Elizabeth Cady Stanton

Barking. Definitely barking. I take the steps two at a time, hearing a wop-like something hit the door head on and a desperate scratching until the door opens, and then he tackles me, all hundred and something pounds of golden polar bear fur and goofy smile and sloppy kisses and salty seaweed smell.

"Salty," I sob, hugging him tight. "Oh my gosh, I missed you so much! Thank God you're all right." I look up through eyes swimming with tears to see my grandmother standing there. "Nana!" I jump up to hug her.

"Hello, sweetheart. I told you not to worry."

"Oh, Nana, it's so good to see you. Thank you for finding him."

Salty is barking at Rob. "It's okay, Salty. He's our friend."

"Hi, buddy," Rob gets on his knees, let's Salty check him out. He ruffles the fur on Salty's head with his knuckles. "So this is the famous Salty Dog. I've heard a lot about you. Welcome to Troy, buddy. Wait until Josie sees *you*."

Ruff, ruff. Salty looks at me for confirmation.

Yep, we like this guy, I tell him with a smile and a nod.

"Show Rob how you smile, Salty." I demonstrate. "Come on, show him."

Salty Dog smiles.

"Maybe he can teach Garfield that trick," Rob says. "He's such a grumpy cat."

*****

Rob leaves, and I walk Salty out the side door to find a good "potty" spot. Nana brought food and water dishes, a bag of the kibble we serve him, a new comfy toy, a blue dinosaur, and a gift box from No Mutts About It—a deluxe grooming supplies kit and year's worth of treats.

Salty sniffs all around the house, then yawns and lies right next to my closed door. There's no question where this dog is sleeping tonight. Right beside me with my arms around his neck.

Best night ever.

*****

Early the next morning, Nana and I are having tea with milk, just the way we like it. We're sitting on the kitchen couch, looking out at the yard, Salty's head resting on my foot like an oversized fuzzy slipper. I get my early-bird gene from Nana. Salty acquired his from me.

"Oh, Nana, I'm so happy you're here!" I take her hand and squeeze it.

"Me, too, sweetheart, me too."

"Tell me again what happened." I was so busy playing with my dog last night that I missed the details of Salty's rescue that she shared with Mom and Sam.

"The woman is mentally ill. The fire chief thinks she's suffering from dementia. She was driving past No Mutts About It the night of the fire, and she thought that Salty was her dog, Pumpkin Pie, that she had lost as a child."

"Pumpkin Pie?" I ask. Salty whimpers at the name. "Don't worry." I hug him. "We know you're Salty Dog."

"She lured Salty into her car somehow," Nana continues.

"Most likely with food," I say, feeding Salty another dog treat, then another, rubbing his head, kissing his wet nose. "And Salty was spooked from the fireworks that night and probably wanted to get away from the noise."

"Well, anyway," Nana says, "she took him to her house. The police officer who followed up on the lead said the lady was taking good care of him. Had a nice enclosed yard. Bought him lots of toys. She wasn't trying to steal him. She really thought he was Pumpkin Pie."

Salty looks up at me and his eyes wince.

"Sorry, buddy. That's the last time *ever* those words will be uttered in this house."

"That may be a problem come Thanksgiving," Nana says, and we laugh.

Nana sips her tea. "This is a beautiful house, don't you think?" She looks at me pointedly.

"The town is beautiful, too." I tell her about my adventures exploring and about the Key Club girls.

Nana locks eyes with me and smiles. She sets down her tea. "Give me a hug, shmug. You have such a kind heart."

Mom comes up behind us. "How about we go out for breakfast?"

"Sounds good, dear," Nana says. "Look," she points at the birdfeeder. "A cardinal."

I smile at the bright red bird. Of course, Gramp visits when Nana is here.

"And there's his mate up on that branch." She points to the red-and-brown feathered female, much less attractive than her partner.

"Why are the males prettier?" I ask.

"It's an ego thing," Mom jokes.

"Now, now," Sam says, joining us. "We're not all like that."

Chapter 32
The Key Club Girls

*I would have girls regard themselves not as
adjectives, but as nouns.*

—Elizabeth Cady Stanton

Saturday is finally here! Four copies of *Sunny Holiday*, check. Four
journals and pens, check. Four bags of Nana's candy, check. Club
notebook, music, check, check, check.

I bike down Middleburgh and turn left on River Street, past the
Roots and Urban Grow Center. Downtown, I wave and say, "Hi, Sam," to
the silver statue by the bus stop. Will I see the real Uncle Sam again? I'm
curious to know more about him. Did he think of himself as patriotic?
Does he like being an American icon?

Veering onto Second Street, I bike down a few blocks, pausing to
read the names of famous composers—Beethoven…Mozart…Chopin—
engraved along the roofline of the famous Troy Music Hall. Then it's
left onto State Street where I see PFEIL'S Hardware Store. There's a
colorful display of gardening tools and bird feeders in the front windows,
reminding me of my sunflowers. I hope my seeds sprout soon.

I swing my bike around to look across the street to Barker Park
and gasp. There are the three girls from last Saturday—and about a dozen
others, too.

"She's here!" Braids shouts.

Cinderella runs up and hugs my waist so hard I nearly fall off my bike. I
dismount, and she grabs my hand, pulling me toward the group. "This is
Willa. My *friend*, Willa."

The girls are all different, with one thing in common. They are all
staring at me.

"These girls want to join the club," Bracelets says.

"Great! The more, the merrier. Let's go over there." I walk to the
flat, shady grassy area in the corner and sit down. Cinderella claims the

181

spot on my right. Braids sits on my left.

"Make a circle please, girls, so we can all see each other."

There's a bit of jockeying for positions, some girls insisting on certain spots.

"Let's start with introductions." I open the notebook. "Say your first name, loudly so we can all hear, and spell it for me. Tell us your age and where you go to school."

"What kind of a club is it going to be?" a girl asks.

"Good question. We'll talk about that in a minute. Let's meet everyone first."

"What's the club called?" another girl shouts.

"Well, one person suggested maybe the Key Club Girls," I say, "but...."

"We got keys last week," Braids says, holding hers up to show.

"I'll bring keys for everyone next week." *Someone's got to have some old ones they'd be willing to donate to a good cause.*

"I'd really like to learn all of your names." I start. "My name is Willa. I'm almost fifteen. I go to Troy High School." I purposefully turn to Cinderella next. I nod at her and smile. "Your turn."

"I'm Cinderella."

I keep my eyes focused on her, smiling and nodding encouragingly. "Great," I print her name in the notebook. "Go ahead."

"I'm ten and I'm in fourth grade at School 2."

"School 2? I jogged by there. You have the murals and beautiful sunflowers."

"I love sunflowers," she says.

Bracelets is next. "My name is Ashleigh —A, s, h, l, *E, I, G, H.* I'm ten. I go to Carroll Hill Elementary."

They continue around the circle....

Belinda, 10, School 2
Yamillet, 9, School 2
Makenzee, 10, Carroll Hill
Xylia, 12, Troy Middle School

Fernanda, 11, Carroll Hill

Imani, 10, School 2.

Sara…Brianna…La'Asia…Gisnelys…Yanelys…Maya…Wisdom…Hannah…Kathina, each girl introduces herself.

Braids is last. "Brooklyn, spelled like the place I was born. I am ten-and-a-half, and I go to School 2. The one with the sunflowers."

"Well done, everyone. First off, I want to thank Cinderella, Ashleigh, and Brooklyn, for making me feel so welcome in Troy on the very first day I arrived here." Each member of the trio grins. "Second of all, I have some very exciting news." I tell them about our meeting with the mayor on Tuesday. "You'll get to show him your presentation for the clubhouse."

"You got us a meeting with the *mayor?*" Cinderella's eyes have grown twice their normal size.

"He's important," one of the new girls almost-whispers.

"So are you girls!" I turn on Alicia Keys' "Girl on Fire." Many of them know the words. "She's just a girl but she's on fire…" We sing and dance through a couple of songs before I turn the volume down.

"So what's our club going to be like?" Imani calls out.

"Well…I thought we could discuss books we're reading, write in our journals, talk, listen to music, maybe go for a walk. Is there a trail near here?"

"There's the Eighth Street bike path by my school," Cinderella says.

"I saw that." All bumpy with potholes and weeds, no benches or water fountains.

"Do we have to exercise?" Brianna says. "I don't want to."

"It will be fun," I say.

There are disbelieving groans.

"What about the candy?" Maya asks.

"I brought some today, a few pieces each from my grandmother's store."

"I could bring cookies next time," Brooklyn offers.

"That would be great, Brooklyn, thank you."

I don't have books and journals for all of them. "How about we go around the circle again, and this time tell us about a book you *love*."

I turn to Brooklyn. "You're up first, Miss Brooklyn."

A few minutes later, the circle closes back with me.

"I have so many favorite books. I'll mention two I just finished reading."

When the girls hear about Malala Yousafzai, several of them gasp.

"She's so brave," Xylia says.

When I tell them about Senator Gillibrand, who lives *right here in Troy like us*, Wisdom says, "We should invite her to our club."

"What's our club's name?" Yanelys asks.

"I like the Key Club Girls," Ashleigh says.

"How about The Beautiful Girls?" Fernanda suggests.

"No," Yamillet says. "We're not that."

"*Yes, you are.*" I point to each girl and look into her eyes as I make my way around the circle. "You are smart, bold, beautiful, powerful girls, every single one of you."

A few of the girls giggle.

"Just don't call us the Troylits," Cinderella says.

"What?"

"Like toilet. Sometimes people say that to put us down. Like Troy girls are no good."

"That's awful," I say. "Let's change that to mean Troy-*Lit*. Lit up with good ideas. I'm still a fan of the Key Club Girls, but I want it to be your decision."

"How about we vote?" Brooklyn says.

"Good suggestion," I say.

Brooklyn takes charge. "Okay, how many vote Key Club Girls?"

Almost everyone raises their hand.

"How many vote Troy-Lit?" There are a few hands.

"Majority rules," I say. "Congratulations, Key Club Girls. You've made your first official group decision."

"Key Club Girls! Wooohoooo!" Brooklyn shoves her fist in the air. The girls clap and cheer.

"Can we have a mascot?" Sara asks.

"How about a lion?" Cinderella says quietly.

"How about a koala?" Makenzee suggests.

"Or a dolphin," Fernanda says.

"No," Hannah says. "School Fourteen already has the dolphin."

"I think a lion is a great choice," I say. "What made you suggest that, Cinderella?"

"Do you know those two lion heads on Second Street…"

"Yes." I tell them about the little girl with the library books. I make a paw and roar like she did.

"I always stick my hand in the lions' mouths, too," Fernanda says.

"Me, too," says Wisdom.

"Me, too," other girls say.

"I love the idea of a lion mascot," I say. "Lions are noble creatures. But when you have something to say that you truly believe in, I don't want you to roar like a lion; I want you to roar like a girl—heart-smart and loud-proud."

"She's funny," Xylia says.

I hand the bags of candy to Cinderella, Imani, and Ashleigh, asking them to distribute it equally. "Now that you've decided on a name, what do you think we need to do to get ready for our meeting on Tuesday?" Hands pop up all over the circle.

"We could make a poster!"

"We should make up a cheer. That's how they'll remember us."

"I don't think anyone will be able to forget you girls," I say as I unwrap a bright pink toffee.

"No matter what we do, Willa," Ashleigh says, "we still won't be able to vote."

"Maybe. But if we don't use our voices and speak up, it's nobody's fault but our own." The hour goes by quickly. Brooklyn and Imani take on leadership roles naturally, deciding that, since we have limited supplies today, the most important thing is that the mayor knows *why* Key Club Girls need a clubhouse. "Can everyone come up with at least one reason?"

They break off into small groups to talk about it, and when they're done, Fernanda suggests everyone practice standing up and talking. "Because sometimes it's scary to talk loudly in front of people," she explains.

Each of the girls stands in front of the group and talks about why they'd like a clubhouse. They bring up all sorts of reasons, many I'd never even thought of:

"We've always lived in apartments, and I've never gotten to decorate my room. A clubhouse would be a place I could."

"The homework club at my afterschool program is really crowded, and it's hard for me to concentrate. The clubhouse would be quieter because there would be fewer of us."

"A clubhouse would be *ours!*" says Cinderella, roaring loudest of all.

I look at all of the girls. "You did a great job roaring. I know the mayor is going to be impressed." I look at my watch, sad to tell them we've got to wrap up. "How about a cheer to conclude the first official meeting of the Key Club Girls?"

"Yes!"

"Let's make a circle. Your line is 'Heart Smart and Loud Proud.' Ready?"

"Yes!"

"Don't roar like a lion; Roar like a girl. How's a girl roar?"

"Heart Smart and Loud Proud."

"How's girl roar?"

"Heart Smart and Loud Proud."

"How's a girl roar?"

"HEART SMART and LOUD PROUD!"

Chapter 33
Best Kept Secret

My world has changed but I have not.
—Malala Yousafzai

Late Saturday afternoon, Rob texts to see if I want to go for a walk with him in Frear Park. "There's a place I want to show you."

Perfect, I think after I send my answer. *Now I can ask him about the dance.*

Salty's still on my bed, and he looks up at me with his best smile. "Sorry, Salty. You stay here." I scratch him behind the ears and his tail thumps even louder. "This time."

Rob's sitting on his front porch waiting for me. He's wearing black sweatpants and a red hoodie with the Albany Academy logo. I'm wearing gray sweatpants and a purple hoodie with the Troy High seal.

"Already showing your school spirit," he says. "Nice. You start Monday, right?"

"Yep."

"Excited?"

"Yes. And a little nervous, too."

"You'll be fine," Rob smiles. "Everybody's going to love you."

"Do you want to go to Homecoming with me?" I blurt it out quickly.

"The game?" he asks.

I stop and look at him. "And the dance...*both*."

He smiles. "Sure, okay."

"Wonderful." *What now?* With JFK, everything sort of fell into place. And he was always the one asking me out, at least in the beginning.

"Did you ask me out on our first date?" Rob asks.

"Second. You're forgetting about the ice cream."

"That was just a friendly welcome-to-the-neighborhood gesture," Rob says.

"Really?"

"No way." We laugh.

There's a golden hue over the landscape, a cooler breeze, leaves changing colors. I take a deep breath. "Do you smell that, Rob? That's fall, my favorite season."

"Mine, too," he says.

We pass the playground and tennis courts. I slip my hand into his, trying to be casual as I point out the old shed.

"That's the building my girls want for a clubhouse."

"Oh, so they're 'your girls' now?"

I elbow him.

"This is Bradley Lake," Rob says, turning onto a narrow path along the water.

"I didn't realize there were trails here."

"A lot of people don't." The path is rough-going in parts, tree roots bulging up, a fallen limb. "Look at the turtle on the log," Rob points.

I stop and bend down to get a closer look. Slowly, careful not to disturb him or anyone who might be inside the log, I pull out my phone to take a picture. "Can you take one of the two of us?" I point at the turtle. Rob takes my phone, and I make a shocked "Oh my goodness it's a turtle!!" face.

"Yep, that's one for the books," he shows me the picture. I can't wait to send it to Tina, with a little bit of Rob-related backstory. I don't even mind that she'll tell all of Bramble.

We keep walking.

There's a tricky spot where we have to leap from one stepping stone to another over a wet marshy area. Now we are in the woods. I hear water gushing. The path steepens. I take short quick steps to keep from sliding, following Rob's lead.

There's a stream to the right of us, the whooshing sound growing louder. "Here it is." Rob steps aside, giving me a full view of a small but beautiful waterfall. "A waterfall hidden in the heart of Troy."

"Wow," is all I can manage to say. It's a picture-perfect scene. We stand there appreciating.

"It's the best kept secret," he says. "All the times I've come here I've never seen anyone else around."

I close my eyes to savor this moment. When I open them, he's looking at me. He smiles and I smile right back.

So this is what it feels like when your heart wakes.

We follow the trail to the top of the golf course, pause to look out over the city.

I used to sit up on the bluff and look out over the ocean.

This, too, is beautiful.

"Nice view, huh?" Rob says. "This is where we come to watch the fireworks."

Joy rises inside.

"Come on, I'll race you!" Laughing, I tear off down the hill, running like a girl who's ready to roar.

And when that boy finally catches up with me, this girl just might give him a kiss.

Chapter 34
First Day Jitters

Far away there in the sunshine are my highest aspirations. I may not reach them, but I can look up and see their beauty, believe in them, and try to follow where they lead.

—Louisa May Alcott

Monday morning comes faster than I can believe. Before I know it, I'm sitting in the kitchen, having a pre-first-day-at-a-new-school breakfast with Sam as Mom heads out the door. "Are you *sure* you don't want me to stay and drive you? I feel bad leaving you on your first day at a new school."

I wave her out the door. "You aren't leaving me. I mean, you are, but I'll be fine. I have been to school before."

She laughs and nervously smooths her deep blue blazer. "Okay, one last check before I go: how do I look?"

"Beautiful," Sam says admiringly.

"Powerful," I add. "Good luck!"

"You, too!" she calls over her shoulder before she closes the door behind her.

"I'm so glad Mom decided to go to this event with Penny." Mom was such a big hit at the luncheon that Penny asked her to come to a second event for New York Businesswomen. It's this afternoon, but Mom has to take the train to Albany.

"Me, too," Sam takes our dishes to the sink and rinses them. "I have to ask again: are you sure you don't want a ride to school?"

"Yes, I am sure. I want to treat it like any other day. Making it special will only make me more nervous." I glance at the clock. "I better finish getting ready. Don't want to be late!"

I put on the outfit I chose last night—simple jeans and a pink t-shirt, with a jacket Tina picked out—and lace up my pink sneakers. I wanted to run to school, but Sam pointed out that will quickly get hard with books and supplies. So he bought me a basket to attach to Dr. Craig's bike, and Mom promised to take me shopping for a bike of my own next weekend.

I wave goodbye to Sam, who gives me a good-luck hug, and wheel the bike out of the garage. It's already a beautiful day.

The ride is over far too fast. It feels like only seconds have gone by since I started down the driveway, and now I'm locking up my bike in front of the school. It will have a lot of good company—the rack is already filling up with an assortment of bikes and it's still early.

I take a deep breath. *Don't be such a scaredy-cat,* I tell myself as I walk through the heavy double doors. *It's not like you've never done this before.* But my hands are still shaking when I get to my locker.

I have no idea where people hang out before classes, so I decide to go to homeroom. Of course, I'm the only person there, but I take it as a chance to write in the journal Mom gave me. Yesterday, I started a list of things I could do to help the Key Club Girls at their presentation tomorrow, like bringing small water bottles and making sure to give them all a key before they go in to talk to the mayor. *Your very own key to the city.* They're going to do great things and tomorrow's only the beginning.

Alaina pops her head in a few minutes later. "Hey, I thought I'd find you here. Settling in okay? Need anything?"

It's so nice to see a familiar face, even if I spent only a few minutes with her last week. "Everything is great. I found my locker, and I found this room, so I think I'm off to a good start."

"Your last school was a lot smaller, huh?"

"Is it that obvious?" We both laugh.

"It's okay, you'll get used to it here." She walks in and hands me a map with different color highlighter marks on different classrooms. "I made you a map. Campus gets a lot smaller once you realize that things are pretty much organized by subject. See?" She points to six rooms in a row that are circled in bright green. "Those are all the science classrooms. Green because you know, the Hulk, mad scientists."

I keep looking at the map while she explains the other colors—purple for art and drama, yellow for math, orange for English and Debate. I point to a big pink star. "What's that?"

"That is where you're going to meet me for lunch. I made sure Mr. Riccio put us on the same track so we can have lunch together." I give her a confused look. "Half the school has lunch first, then the other half. The caf would *technically* fit us all, but my mom says that's how they did it when she went here and you couldn't even hear yourself think. Lunch is pretty mellow, but I didn't want you to have to sit by yourself. Unless," she pauses, "you're more of an alone person? My feelings will not be hurt if you are."

I shake my head. "Definitely not. Thank you so much, Alaina."

"It's nothing. My friends are all excited to meet you, anyway." The bell rings and she taps her finger on the pink star again. "Lunch. Don't forget."

How could I? I can't help but sigh a tiny sigh as she walks out of the room and classmates start pouring in. *Okay, Willa, time to roar.*

*****

The first half of the day goes by in a blur. I start with Global History, and it goes well. Then on to Honors English, my favorite class, of course. Even break went by in a blur: run to my locker to put books away, grab new books, make sure not to lose Alaina's amazing map, and only get lost once on my way to Accelerated Math.

Now it's lunch time. The number of students in the hall seems to triple as they all go to the same place, and I can't believe that this is only half the school. Finally, I see Alaina wave me over to a group of girls.

"You made it! I was getting a little worried about you. Okay," she straightens her backpack, "introductions. Girls, this is the new girl I was telling you about. Her name's Willa, and we're going to make sure she has a great first week at Troy, okay?" Five girls smile back at me, all seeming friendly, though a couple might be shy. "Willa, these are the girls. That's

Lisa," a tall girl gives a huge grin and waves, "Gabrielle," one of the shy girls gives a quick wave, "Toni," braids even longer than Brooklyn's, "and research shows that you can't remember more than three names at a time, so I'll wait until after we eat to tell you the rest."

"You're always making stuff up," one of the unnamed girls teases Alaina.

Toni stares at me. "Do I know you?"

"Well, I don't know *you*, so I don't think it's very likely." We get in a long but moving line. "I just moved here last week."

She looks up at the ceiling, trying to remember. "Oh! Are you the Willa who had the Key Club Girls meeting this weekend?"

"Oh my gosh, yes!"

"You know Brooklyn? That's my little sister. She hasn't talked about anything but you and that club for the last three days." A few of the other girls chime in that they have cousins in the group or have heard of the club. "If you ever need any help, let me know. I taught at the community center this summer, and I had a lot of fun."

"I'd love some help. I'm sort of making it up as I go along," I confess. "They were just in the park at the same time I was, and we got to talking, and they told me about the clubhouse. And now there's a club that's sort of about books and girl power. Obviously," I laugh, "I could use any help I can get."

"I was thinking about trying to put together a youth committee for taking care of neighborhood parks," Gabrielle says softly from behind me. "Do you think the girls would be interested?"

"Maybe." In my mind, I'm sure the girls would love to be a part of a project like that, but I don't want to get in the habit of speaking for them. "Why don't you both come to our next meeting, and you can ask them yourself? We have an appointment with the mayor tomorrow after school" —a couple of the girls' eyes go wide—, "and then we're meeting every Saturday at two." Toni, Gabrielle, and a couple of the other girls say they'll come.

Alaina is grinning at me. "I knew you'd get along fine here," she says as she walks back to class with me. We both have Living Environment next and then I'll finish the day with French Three while she goes to Spanish.

"I've never had Madame Dauphine," Alaina tells me before we part ways, "but Gabri had her last year and she told me to tell you"—she reads off her phone—"'Madame seems mean at first, but she really wants her students to work hard and learn. Don't be scared, she's very sweet.' I hope that helps?" She gives me a quick hug. "Good luck and I'll see you tomorrow!"

I walk into Madame Dauphine's classroom actually pretty excited. I've always liked teachers who have high expectations for their students. It pushes the class to be better, and I always learn a lot in classes like that. I'd like to think if I ever taught, I'd be like that, but Sam says I'm too nice to be that strict. Maybe working with the Key Club Girls will help me with that, learn to balance sweet with strict.

*****

Sam knocks on my door when he gets home from the college. "Stella called to say she's going to be late, so it's just you and me for dinner. Amante's isn't too crowded, and you can tell me all about your first day at Troy High?"

"As long as there's pineapple."

"I am hurt that you would think I could ever forget your favorite pizza, Willa." Sam puts his hand over his heart and puts on his best fake pout. "Are you starving? I'm starving."

"Let's go now, then."

The pizza place isn't too crowded, since it's still early, and it doesn't take long for our pizzas to arrive. Yes, we ordered two pizzas for two people. "Your mom will need leftovers," Sam explains when I make a comment. Now, he grins at his tray full of tomato, olive, and feta-topped slices. "So, down to business. How did your first day go?"

I swallow a delicious bite of Hawaiian pizza and nod. I tell him about my classes and about Alaina and her friends. "I was so excited when Toni said she was Brooklyn's sister!" But I spent more time gushing about Madame Dauphine. "She's amazing, Sam. You'd love her, she's so smart. She was born in Martinique,"—I do my best French accent—"and she's lived all over the world, including the French Rivera, and *Rome*, and Bali. Her classroom walls are covered with posters of old French movies and photographs from places she's lived. She has her *PhD* in French literature. Her class is going to be so hard, but I'm so excited!"

"I can tell."

"She's retired. Gabri told me that Madame Dauphine taught at Princeton and then Bennington and finally came to Troy. She—Madame—said that she had two teachers in high school who changed her life, and she wanted to honor them by giving back."

Sam calls the waiter over and asks for to-go boxes, and I pretend not to notice how little is left of Sam's pizza. When I ask him if he enjoyed his dinner, he grins.

*****

Mom doesn't get home 'til late. I'm already in bed when she knocks on my door and opens it a bit. "Willa?" she whispers. "I don't want to wake you, but I wanted to say I love you, and I hope your first day was great."

"I love you too," I whisper back, "just about to fall asleep."

"We'll talk in the morning," I hear her say as she closes the door.

I roll over and snuggle down into bed, knowing that I need a good night's sleep. Tomorrow we see the mayor!

Chapter 35
Roar

Many persons have a wrong idea of what constitutes true happiness. It is not attained through self-gratification but through fidelity to a worthy purpose.

—Helen Keller

"*Annnnd*, I told Madame Dauphine about the Key Club Girls today, *and* she said she'd love to come talk to them!" Mom is giving me a ride to the mayor's office from school, and we're catching up about my first two days at Troy High.

"I am so glad you have her for a teacher, Willa," Mom says. "You've always liked French. Maybe you'll be an ambassador to France or Belgium."

I think about it for a minute. It could be a lot of fun…. "No, I think politics is still where I could do the most good."

We pull into a spot at City Hall, and Mom gets out of the car with me. "I want to meet these girls of yours," she explains. I agree that she can come along, but only on the condition that she doesn't come into the meeting with us. "I have a book," she says, holding up her own copy of *Off the Sidelines*.

When we get to the front steps, Toni is standing talking to Brooklyn and Cinderella. "I thought they could use the moral support," she tells me. "And you could probably use a helping hand." I introduce her and the girls to my mom. Cinderella comes up and wraps her arms around my waist.

"I told my mom *allllll* about you," she says proudly.

"And I told *my* mom all about you!"

She smiles. She's already getting louder, more talkative. I hope she speaks up in the presentation today.

Almost all the girls are able to make it. Ashleigh and Imani come together, carrying a tri-fold poster board, and another girl—*Wisdom*, I remind myself—is holding a big stack of hand-drawn flyers. A couple couldn't come for various reasons—soccer, babysitting, etc.—but once everyone is accounted for, we wave goodbye to my mom and bustle into the building.

It would be a tight squeeze to get us all in one elevator, so Toni takes up one group while I wait with the second. Cinderella is still by my side, along with Imani and Kathina. I talk to them about their presentation, and Imani opens up the board. "A lot of us worked on it after school yesterday. Brooklyn's mom let us use the whole kitchen table."

"I did the drawings." Cinderella points to a picture of four girls standing next to a broken-down shed. "And then, see, this is how beautiful we'd make it." Then next picture shows the same girls, but now the shed behind them is shiny and new.

"This is amazing, Cinderella. I am so proud of all of you."

"Do you think the mayor's going to like it?" Kathina asks.

"I think he's going to love it."

*****

The mayor walks toward us from behind his desk and shakes hands with each and every girl before the presentation, including Toni and me. During the presentation, he sits quietly, his hands folded in his lap, while the girls show him their charts and drawings. They had thought of everything. They even had scraps of fabric showing what they wanted the curtains to look like.

I am so proud of them.

"This is a very impressive presentation," he says when they are done. "I want you to know that I am very proud to be the mayor of a town that has such smart and innovative young people. Troy is lucky to have the Key Club Girls." The girls all had huge smiles plastered on their faces. A few hugged each other, and there were quite a few high fives.

"Does that mean we can have the clubhouse?" Cinderella asks. With the other girls' encouragement, she found the courage to roar *twice* during the presentation. I can't help but be extra proud of her.

The mayor sits down and puts his hands together. "No." The girls' reactions are audible, but the mayor holds up his hand. "Unfortunately, that building is being renovated with endowed monies expressly designated for that project. But, I happen to know that there are several other vacant buildings downtown that we are hoping to restore. I think some of them might be an even *better* fit than the old shed."

Now the Key Club Girls are ecstatic. The mayor invites all of us to the next City Council meeting, where Key Club Girls will present its plan for building renovation and the council will decide *which* building to give them. "What if they change their minds?" Makenzee asks.

The mayor shakes his head. "Impossible. You have the mayor's seal of approval. You will most definitely get a clubhouse." Cinderella and Kathina run up and hug the mayor. He's still got a big goofy smile on his face after we've picked everything up and are headed toward the door.

*****

Outside, Toni and I gather the girls for one last Key Club Girls Cheer. I wave my mom over, and the girls love teaching her the cheer. Our voices echo out from city hall to the whole downtown:

"Ready?"

"Yes!"

"Don't roar like a lion; Roar like a girl. How's a girl roar?"

"Heart Smart and Loud Proud."

"How's a girl roar?"

"Heart Smart and Loud Proud."

"How's a girl roar?"

"HEART SMART and LOUD PROUD!"

*****

The girls leave slowly, in groups of two or three, still bubbling with excitement over their big win. Toni gives me a quick hug before she leaves with Brooklyn.

"Brooklyn's going to be talking about this for weeks. If she gets too annoying, I'm sending her to you," says Toni. Brooklyn looks ecstatic at the thought.

I laugh and my mom crouches down to look Brooklyn in the eyes. "We would love to have any of you over, anytime. If *she* gets too annoying, you come on over, okay?" Brooklyn and Stella shake hands seriously, while Toni rolls her eyes.

I wave as the last group of girls disappears around the corner. I can't stop smiling, I'm so full of pride for all of them.

I think about the last week.

The Inn and leaving Bramble...

Arriving in Troy, wanting to hate it but falling in love with the city...

Meeting the girls, starting the Key Club...

New school, new friends, maybe a new boyfriend...

So much has changed....

I have, too....

Yet I am still *me*...Willa.

I think of that acrostic poem. Who knows if I will be Willa the Wedding Planner ever again, or Willa in the White House, president someday.

But I will always be me. **A**lways Willa.

*****

WILLA'S PIX LIST

Willa is a self-described "book lover," aka bibliophile. Here are a few she recommends:

Almond, David	*My Name is Mina*
Anderson, Laurie Halse	*Speak*
Applegate, Katherine	*The One and Only Ivan*
Appelt, Kathi	*Keeper*
Birdsall, Jeanne	*The Penderwicks*
Collins, Suzanne	*The Hunger Games*
Cleave, Chris	*Little Bee*
DiCamillo, Kate	*The Magician's Elephant*
Erskine, Kathryn	*Mockingbird*
Gillibrand, Kirsten	*Off the Sidelines*
Green, John	*The Fault in Our Stars*
Grimes, Nikki	*The Road to Paris*
Hale, Shannon	*Princess Academy*
Holm, Jennifer	*Turtle in Paradise*
Kyle, Aryn	*The God of Animals*
Levithan, David	*Boy Meets Boy*
Martin, Ann M.	*Rain, Reign*
Palacio, R.J.	*Wonder*
Pearson, Mary E.	*A Room on Lorelei Street*
Rowell, Rainbow	*Eleanor & Park*
Spinelli, Jerry	*Stargirl*
Williams-Garcia, Rita	*One Crazy Summer*
Yousafzai, Malala	*I Am Malala*
Zusak, Markus	*The Book Thief*

Each Willa book contains a "Willa's Pix" list of recommendations. For a complete list of all the titles, check out www.coleenparatore.com.

SPARK-STARTERS FOR DISCUSSIONS OR WRITING

True change takes place in the imagination.
—Thomas Moore

1. Is there a major change you have faced in your life? What was positive/negative about that?

2. Have you experienced a traumatic event such as the devastating fire at the Bramble Inn?

3. Have you ever lost a pet?

4. Do you keep a journal?

5. When you are being "exactly yourself," how would your friends or family describe you?

6. If you've ever moved to a new city or neighborhood, what was that like?

7. How about a new school?

8. Who are the women role models in your life? What traits in them do you admire?

9. Name a book you love and why.

10. What do you think the legal voting age in our country should be?

11. Willa doesn't like to be referred to as a "guy"—do you think pronouns matter?

12. What is an issue you have a strong opinion about? What do you want to roar about?

13. What do you think the Key Club Girls will do with their new clubhouse? What would you do if you could have a clubhouse for girls in your town?

14. What do you think will happen next in Willa's life?

15. What would you like to have happen next in your own life?

ACKNOWLEDGMENTS

With sincerest thanks to: my assistant, Jamie Holmes; editor, Jennifer Rees; Laura Mancuso, Lee Wind, Leslie Iorillo, Rana DiOrio, and the entire team at Little Pickle Press; the Troy City Schools community, students, teachers, and staff, especially Patti Weaver, Mary Grace Tompkins, Daniel Hayes, and Troy Middle School Library Media Specialist, Nancy Serson; Rensselaer County Historian, Kathy Sheehan; the many Troy girls who shared ideas, opinions, and energy with me, especially Hannah, Marisa, Samantha, Shawanna, Alexis, Aaliyah, Makiah, Gabrielle, Emily, Hannah, Danysha, Juliana, Gennavive, Jenna, Farriya, Quyana, Celia, and Miya; my sons, Dylan, Connor, and Christopher Paratore for unwavering love and support; my beloved mother, Peg Spain Murtagh, forever my greatest teacher and guiding light; my brother, Jerry Murtagh for the "pink notebook" and for his rock-solid belief in me and my writing; my fiancé, Columbus Buish, Sr., for filling my life with love, lyrics, and laughter; and to every Willa fan, past and future…keep roaring like a girl—heart-smart and loud-proud.

AUTHOR BIO

Coleen Murtagh Paratore is the award-winning author of more than twenty books. Her debut novel, *The Wedding Planner's Daughter* (Simon & Schuster, 2004), has sold more than a half million copies internationally, was twice optioned for a movie, and sparked the *Willa* books—enjoyed by fans young and old for more than a decade now. She is a popular presenter at schools, conferences, and literary events, where she inspires others to "catch ideas like fireflies on a summer night and write what only YOU can write." Coleen teaches public speaking at The Sage Colleges, Albany and Troy, NY; leads writing workshops at The Arts Center of the Capital Region, Troy, NY; and coaches writing clients. As a life-long believer in paying "community rent," Coleen donates time to Girls, Inc. of the Greater Capital Region; Literacy Volunteers of Rensselaer County; the YWCA of the Greater Capital Region; Rutger's University Council on Children's Literature; Girls on the Run; and Joseph's House & Shelter for the Homeless. Proud mother of three adult sons, Christopher, Connor, and Dylan Paratore, Coleen lives in Troy, NY, with her beloved Columbus Buish, Sr., and enjoys weekends at "While-Away," their lake house near the Vermont border, where cell connection is sketchy, but the bird watching and book reading are blissful.

Visit the author at *www.coleenparatore.com*.

OUR MISSION

Little Pickle Press is dedicated to creating media that fosters kindness in young people—and doing so in a manner congruent with that mission.

Little Pickle Press
Environmental Benefits Statement

This book is printed on BPM Inc. Envirographic™ 100 paper. Made in the USA, it is the recipient of the Governor's Award of Excellence in Energy Efficiency. It is made with 100% PCRF (Post-Consumer Recovered Fiber) collected in North America. It is FSC®-certified, acid-free, and 100% Process Chlorine-Free Certified.

Little Pickle Press saved the following resources by using Envirographic™ 100 paper:

trees	energy	greenhouse gases	wastewater	solid waste
Post-consumer recovered fiber displaces wood fiber with savings translated as trees.	PCRF content displaces energy used to process equivalent virgin fiber.	Measured in CO_2 equivalents, PCRF content and Green Power reduce greenhouse gas emissions.	PCRF content eliminates wastewater needed to process equivalent virgin fiber.	PCRF content eliminates solid waste generated by producing an equivalent amount of virgin fiber through the pulp and paper manufacturing process.
77 trees	**34 mil BTUs**	**6,620 lbs**	**35,906 gal**	**2,404 lbs**

Calculations based on research by Environmental Defense Fund and other members of the Paper Task Force and applies to print quanities of 7,500 books.

B Corporations are a new type of company that use the power of business to solve social and environmental problems. Little Pickle Press is proud to be a Certified B Corporation.